Praise for Olen Steinhauer

"Steinhauer has been likened to John le Carré and rightly so."
—*The Washington Post*

"[Steinhauer has] been called John le Carré's heir apparent, and the best espionage writer of his generation."
—CNN

"Mr. Steinhauer draws his spies as flesh-and-blood characters in whom his readers invest both attention and emotion."
—Janet Maslin, *The New York Times*

"One of the hottest names in spy fiction today . . . Entertaining."
—*USA Today*

"Olen Steinhauer is not afraid to challenge readers. . . . Much like John le Carré, Steinhauer doesn't offer simple answers. In his books, the good guys are elusive and the shadowy world his characters inhabit is blanketed in shades of gray. If you've never read one of his stories, dive in. But don't get comfortable. It's going to be a wild ride."
—*Star Tribune*

"Olen Steinhauer is among the best contemporary espionage writers."
—*The Seattle Times*

All the Old Knives

"A splendid tour de force . . . Without neglecting the turmoil of the geopolitical landscape, the novel focuses more intensely on the equally treacherous landscapes of the human heart." —*The Washington Post*

"[A] sneaky little gem . . . Mr. Steinhauer sustains the difficult balancing act of melding a heart-racing espionage plot with credible dinner table conversation. . . . Mr. Steinhauer specializes in tough showdowns. And the more innocently they begin, the more devastatingly they end."

—*The New York Times Book Review*

"Most of *All the Old Knives* revolves around Pelham and Favreau's dinner, and the fact that the book moves so swiftly and alluringly is a testament to Steinhauer's skills as an entertainer. He stretches considerable tension across an entire book, rather than a handful of swift scenes, and it's gratifying to watch him do something so daringly retro and contrary to what we've come to expect in a thriller."

—*Richmond Times-Dispatch*

"*All the Old Knives* is a love story hauntingly set in the framework of a terrorist attack aboard a plane at the airport in Vienna. . . . Mr. Steinhauer is an expert at twists and turns, all the more riveting for their truth."

—*The Washington Times*

"It's not news that Olen Steinhauer is among the best contemporary espionage writers, and *All the Old Knives* confirms it. If you're a fan of intelligent spy novels that don't need much bang-bang, details about ordnance, or people who save the world single-handedly, this one's for you."
—*The Seattle Times*

"There's great narrative energy in the thrust and counter-thrust of the dinner conversation, as well as in the re-creation of the Viennese events; Steinhauer is a very fine writer and an excellent observer of human nature, shrewd about the pleasures and perils of spying."
—*Publishers Weekly* (starred review)

"Readers hooked on the jolt of adrenaline that typically accompanies Steinhauer's intelligent thrillers needn't fear the highfalutin backstory; though this does essentially take place over the course of a single meal, it delivers intrigue, suspense, and a heart-stopping finale. . . . You'll devour it in one night."
—*Booklist* (starred review)

"[A] masterfully plotted and suspenseful standalone . . . It's an understatement to say that nothing is as it seems, but even readers well versed in espionage fiction will be pleasantly surprised by Steinhauer's plot twists and double backs."
—*Kirkus Reviews* (starred review)

"This genre-bending spy novel takes Hitchcockian suspense to new heights. Over the course of a meal, with flashbacks, the eternal questions of trust, loyalty, and authentic love are deftly dissected. Readers drawn to the story of a loving couple trapped in a terrible embrace will be thrilled to follow Henry and Celia's tortured pas de deux." —*Library Journal* (starred review)

The Milo Weaver Novels

"[Milo Weaver's] company is at least as valuable to the series' appeal as is his flair for international trickery."

—Janet Maslin, *The New York Times*

"Olen Steinhauer's Milo Weaver novels are must-reads for lovers of the genre." —*The Washington Post*

"Like le Carré's George Smiley, Weaver is a richly imagined creation with a scarred psyche and a complex backstory that elevates him above the status of run-of-the-mill world-weary spook."

—*The New York Times Book Review*

"Olen Steinhauer is one of the most talented of the new generation of spy writers. His characters are nuanced, his story lines rooted in today's headlines but with added zing, like a burst of citrus in a dry martini."

—*Financial Times*

"[Olen Steinhauer] ranks with John le Carré and such other guaranteed masters of spy fiction."

—*Toronto Star*

"Stunning . . . Readers are irresistibly drawn into Weaver's dogged struggle to unravel a complicated game of cat and mouse . . . Steinhauer is at the top of his game—but when isn't he?"

—*USA Today* on *An American Spy*

"*The Nearest Exit* should take its place among the best of the spy thrillers." —Associated Press

"Here's the best spy novel I've ever read that wasn't written by John le Carré."

—Stephen King, *Entertainment Weekly,* on *The Tourist*

ALSO BY OLEN STEINHAUER

The Last Tourist
The Middleman
The Cairo Affair
An American Spy
The Nearest Exit
The Tourist
Victory Square
Liberation Movements
36 Yalta Boulevard
The Confession
The Bridge of Sighs

ALL THE OLD KNIVES

OLEN STEINHAUER

MINOTAUR BOOKS
NEW YORK

This is a work of fiction. All of the characters, organizations, and events portrayed in this novel are either products of the author's imagination or are used fictitiously.

Published in the United States by Minotaur Books, an imprint of St. Martin's Publishing Group

www.minotaurbooks.com

Designed by Anna Gorovoy

The Library of Congress has cataloged the hardcover edition as follows:

Steinhauer, Olen.
All the old knives / Olen Steinhauer.—1st ed.
p. cm.
ISBN 978-1-250-04542-3 (hardcover)
ISBN 978-1-4668-4406-3 (ebook)
I. Title.
PS3619.T4764 A79 2015
813′.6—dc23

2014040117

ISBN 978-1-250-86990-6 (trade paperback)

Our books may be purchased in bulk for promotional, educational, or business use. Please contact your local bookseller or the Macmillan Corporate and Premium Sales Department at 1-800-221-7945, extension 5442, or by email at MacmillanSpecialMarkets@macmillan.com.

First Minotaur Books Trade Paperback Edition: 2022

10 9 8 7 6 5 4 3 2 1

FOR SLAVICA

ACKNOWLEDGMENTS

The seed of this story was planted in California while watching the *Masterpiece* dramatization of Christopher Reid's wonderful poem *The Song of Lunch*. Transfixed by Alan Rickman's and Emma Thompson's performances, I wondered if I could write an espionage tale that took place entirely around a restaurant table. (Not *entirely*, it turned out, but mostly.)

It took time, though. Initially I scribbled some notes before returning to the book at hand (*The Cairo Affair*). A year later, suffering through a blistering August with in-laws in Novi Sad, Serbia, I discovered the old notes. After a year percolating in the unconscious, the story presented itself to me all at once, and when I started typing I couldn't stop. For the next month, I didn't.

Such moments of inspiration are unheard of in my experience, and for a writer to take advantage of them he or she needs an infrastructure of support that allows for a monthlong escape from reality.

So, I want to thank my father-in-law, Gavra Pilić, in whose home this book was composed, and my family, who saw that something odd was going on with me and chose to let me have at it.

HENRY

1

There's a delay taking off from San Francisco— caused, I'm guessing, by an overburdened airport, but no one will tell us for sure. At times like this, sitting stalled on the tarmac, it's easy to think apocalyptically—airports at the bursting point, highways clogged with SUVs helmed by citizens in meltdown, smog alerts and gridlocked emergency rooms, corridors lined with the bleeding. When you're in California this kind of vision explodes into grandiosity, and you imagine the earth ripping apart, spilling all this overconsumption, all the cell phones and seaside villas and hopeful young starlets noisily into the sea. It almost feels like a blessing.

Or maybe it's just me. For all we know, the delay is due to a technical problem. We get over-the-speaker apologies, "thank you for your patience," and occasional attention from already haggard SkyWest stewards who shrug in answer to questions, tossing around "sorry" as if it's the easiest word in the English language. The woman next to me fans herself with a brochure for Presidio Park; redwoods and dense foliage flash, sending a little stale air my way. She says, "Another day, another delay."

"Tell me about it."

"Someone here's bringing bad karma."

I give her a smile, not quite trusting myself to reply out loud.

It's a small plane, an Embraer turboprop that can seat thirty, though on this one there are no more than twenty, all texting whoever's waiting for them in Monterey. My neighbor takes out a phone and thumbs in her own message, something that starts with "U wont believe . . ."

I keep my phone locked away. After fifteen hours flying six thousand miles, then suffering through the mass psychosis of American passport control, the precise time of my arrival feels unimportant.

Were I younger, I might feel differently. International flights used to be a chance to rest up for the coming adventure, but at some point I lost the ability to doze in the air—in 2006, I think, after turning thirty-nine. After . . . well, after the Flughafen. Once you've watched the high-definition video of a hundred and twenty corpses on an airplane, you know you'll never relax again in coach. So by the time I enter California I'm dry with fatigue. My fingers feel shorter and fatter, and my cheeks are alternately warm and cold; a chill sweat periodically soaks my undershirt.

I'm trying not to think too much about planes, and instead look ahead to my destination. Celia Favreau, née Harrison. She will wait, or she won't. For a few minutes, I even convince myself that I don't care. No heartbreak, because at this moment I don't have a heart to break. If she's not at the restaurant, I will simply order a dry martini and some fried shellfish, contemplate civilization's imminent collapse, then head back to the airport for an evening flight back to San Francisco. One last phone call to cover my bases, then fly back to Vienna, where I can finally collapse. I've traveled for too many years, and in far worse conditions, to be unnerved by minor inconveniences. Besides, not having to look her in the eyes would certainly make my job, and my life, a lot easier.

It's four thirty by the time we take off—a half hour late. The propellers whine outside the window as my seatmate pulls out a Kindle. I ask what she's reading, and this leads to a discussion of the virtues and deficits of the contemporary spy novel. She's halfway through an old Len Deighton, in which a hunt for a mole leads the narrator to his own wife. "They just don't make stories like this anymore," she says wistfully. "You knew who the bad guys were back then. These days . . ."

I try to help her out. "Radical Islam?"

"Right. I mean, what kind of an enemy is that?"

An elusive one, I want to say. Again, though, I think better of it.

By the time we land an hour later, I've learned a lot about this woman. Her name is Barbara Jakes. She was raised in Seattle but moved to Monterey with her first husband, who eventually fled to L.A. with a Salinas waitress. After a few months, the waitress abandoned him for a film producer. He still calls, begging for reconciliation, but she has remarried and is now a mother of two sons—holy terrors, she calls them—and works in the health industry.

She reads old thrillers in her spare time and watches NFL football with her boys. She's beginning to suspect her new husband is cheating on her. "You start to wonder," she tells me, "if maybe it's something you're doing that's making them stray."

I shake my head with authority. "Blaming the victim. Don't fall into that trap."

I haven't been in the States for a couple of years, and I've forgotten how readily Americans open up. An hour-long acquaintance, and she's already taking my advice on her emotional health. It seems ludicrous, but perhaps it isn't. Perhaps it's only those who don't know us at all who are able to see us most clearly. Perhaps strangers are our best friends.

In Monterey I catch a glimpse of her husband—a man whose body had been sculpted by soft office chairs, whose casual clothes are made more ridiculous by the addition of a well-worn fanny pack—and from a distance I try to assess the possibility that he's cheating on Barbara. I watch him gather her overnight bag and kiss her briefly on the lips before leading the way out to the parking lot, but I just can't see it. I wonder if Barbara is jumping to conclusions. I wonder if her experiences with her first husband have made her paranoid. I wonder—and I know how much projection is going on—if the scars of her life are beginning to fester, and if they will soon damage those closest to her.

There's only one person ahead of me at the Hertz counter, an overweight businessman, sandpaper scalp, early sixties. I don't remember him from the flight, where I was distracted by Barbara's problems and by not thinking too much about air travel. Now he's disputing the hidden charges for a hatchback—insurance, taxes, fees—and the clerk, a cheery example of California hospitality, explains everything to him as if he were a child. Finally, he stomps off with a new set of keys, lugging only a small shoulder bag. The clerk shows me an opaque smile. "Sir?"

I take a look at their available cars and request a Chevy Impala, but then ask how much for their high-end convertible, a Volvo C70. Twice as much. The clerk waits with Zen-like serenity as I deliberate and finally shrug. "The convertible."

"Yes, sir."

I sign a few papers, use an old Texas driver's license to identify myself, and put everything on my Company card. Soon I'm strolling out under a cloudy October sky, but it's warm enough for me to slip out of my jacket. I use the remote to unlock the car. A few fenders away, the overweight traveler is arguing loudly with someone on his phone as he sits in his idling hatchback, the window up so that I can't make out his words.

I take out my own phone and turn it on. Eventually it connects to AT&T, and a message bleeps. Despite five years and what I've come to do, my heart skips a beat when I see her name on the screen. Turns out I do still have a heart.

You'll be there, right? Text back either way.

I send Celia a single letter—Y—then get into the car. It starts like a dream.

2

From: Henry Pelham *<hpelham@state.gov>*
Date: September 28, 2012
To: Celia Favreau *<celiafavreau@yahoo.com>*
Subject: Hey

C,

I hear from Sarah that you're keeping busy on the West Coast, boosting genius children into the world and making a ruckus of an otherwise quiet enclave. Wien is as it ever was—you're not missing much. Jake says hi. I told him you won't remember him, so please don't pretend you do. Klaus Heller tells me he still owes you some security deposit. Austrians are scrupulously honest, as ever. It's adorable.

How's Drew? There were some whispers of a heart operation, but hopefully they're unfounded. Hanna showed me pics of Evan and Ginny, which were shocking. How does anyone make such adorable children . . . with Drew?? Ginny reminds me of you.

I'm actually going to be in your neck of the woods in a few weeks. Some company thing in Santa Cruz. But I'll have a free day on October 16, a Tuesday, and I'd love to buy you dinner. Name the place, and I'll bill the government. And if you like, I'll ask Klaus for that check. The stars are handing out excellent financial tidings, it seems.

Much love,
H

3

I'm on my own. I feel the truth of this as, roof styl-ishly retracted, I merge onto Highway 1, where trees bloom over the breakdown lanes and, up ahead, the mountains of California's Central Coast loom. In gorgeous landscapes loneliness is more acute—it's something I've noticed. Maybe it's just that there's no one to share the view with you. I don't know.

I turn up the radio. Robert Plant wails about the land of ice and snow.

Though my rental could easily sweep down the road in a handful of minutes, I move to the right and take it easy, the wind gusting in from all sides. It's a comfortable road, so much more accommodating than the roads I've been driving the past decade—the windy, traffic-clogged European lanes where people pull up onto the sidewalk and leave their cars angled, so you have to be a pro to get by without scraping. Also, this road is full of California drivers—easygoing, in no hurry, so unlike European men in their tiny cars, riding your tail in a ridiculous show of machismo. It's easy driving; it feels like an easy life. I can see why she retired here.

Vick said as much in his office up on the embassy's fifth floor, high above Boltzmanngasse. "She's gone," he said. "She's happy. You're wasting your time."

What could I say to that? "I know, Vick. Two kids, after all."

"No, I don't think you do know. I think you're still holding a torch for that woman."

Vick never quite forgave Celia for leaving the station as suddenly as she did, which is why he tends not to say her name anymore. "We're still friends," I said.

Vick laughed. Behind him, a bright Austrian sky filled the window. A plane was riding low, heading toward Flughafen Wien, where in the morning I would be strolling the corridors with my shoulder bag, noticing, as I always did, the Austrian efficiency that had completely airbrushed away the trauma of 2006. "No," Vick said finally. "You *aren't* still friends. That's not how breakups work. And she'll be able to tell, just like I can, that you're still head over heels. After five years, a marriage, and kids, you're the last person she wants to see."

"I think you've got a warped history of romantic entanglements, Vick."

This, at least, provoked a smile. "Let's send Mack. You give him the questions, and he'll bring the answers gift wrapped. You don't need to go."

"Mack won't know if she's lying."

"He's good at his job."

"He doesn't *know* her."

"You don't, either. Not anymore."

I wasn't sure how to rebut that. I couldn't tell him why I needed to go myself, but I at least should have had a ready-made line in my pocket, something rational and irrefutable to throw at him. It's a sign of my eroding capabilities that I had nothing.

He said, "She'll get a restraining order."

"Don't be ridiculous."

"If I were her, I would."

We both let it rest a moment. The plane was gone. I said, "Look, it's an excuse to get out of the basement for a few days. See an old friend. I'll ask her some questions about Frankler, and Uncle Sam can pay for dinner."

"And then you'll wrap it up?" he asked. "Frankler, I mean."

Frankler was the investigation that had kept me in the basement nearly two months, and as I had done plenty of times during our years together, I lied to Vick. "It's tricky. We're trying to cover our asses here—I just want to make sure every inch is covered."

"But you don't have a suspect, right? No actual evidence of wrongdoing?"

"Just one man's word."

"A terrorist's word."

I shrugged.

"And soon afterward he drowned in a pail of water," Vick said. "So it's not like he's going to be taking the stand."

"True."

"Then close it down. Chalk 2006 up to bad luck."

He was even more eager than I was to end this thing.

"I'll find out if Celia has anything to add, and when I get back I'll push on for another week. Okay? Then we'll close it."

"You're eating up our budget, you know."

"Really, Vick? I wander around the basement all day, pulling out old files."

"You fly, too."

"Twice. Over two months I've taken two trips to talk with old hands. Bill Compton and Gene Wilcox. That's hardly extravagant."

He stared at me with those lazy eyes, hesitating, then said, "You ever think about what you'd do if you actually pinned it on someone?"

I had thought about little else. But I said, "Why don't you tell me?"

Vick sighed. I've known him my whole Austrian decade, and he uses sighs the way others crack knuckles or chain-smoke. "You know the score, Henry. We can't afford the embarrassment of a prosecution, and it's not like we're going to do a prisoner swap with the jihadis. Ideally, I wouldn't even want Langley to hear about it."

"So what you're saying is you'd like me to execute the traitor."

He frowned. "I don't believe I said anything of the sort."

We watched each other a moment. I said, "Well, let's hope I don't find anyone to blame it on."

He sighed again and gazed at my hands; I moved them into my pockets. "What does Daniels say?" he asked.

Larry Daniels was the one who'd brought up the theory in the first place. He'd flown in from Langley two months ago in order to have a sit-down with Vick about some new material that had been taken from a prisoner in Gitmo, one Ilyas Shishani, who had been picked up during a raid in Afghanistan. Among the many items he'd spilled, he told the interrogators that the 2006 Vienna Airport disaster had been aided by a source within the U.S. embassy. We'd all been around then—Vick, me, Celia, Gene, and Celia's boss, Bill. After listening to Larry's pitch, Vick had asked me to head the investigation that he'd code-named Frankler.

"Larry's twenty-eight," I reminded him, just as I had when he'd given me Frankler. "He's building a case off of a terrorist's disinformation. He's also desperate to fill his CV."

"Then let's bury it right now. It'll piss off Daniels, but his bosses would be happy to knock him down a few pegs while avoiding a scandal."

It was an idea I'd toyed with for two months. I didn't like Larry Daniels—few who'd met him during his occasional appearances in Vienna did. He was small and itchy to look at, with oily hair and a high, raspy voice. He emanated the conviction that he knew better than anyone else in the room what was going on. But he was also smart, and if I buried Frankler Daniels would dig it up again and dust it off and make a stink. More important, he would take the investigation out of my hands, and that was something I couldn't allow.

I said, "How do you think we'd look once Daniels started shouting around Langley? I've got to follow this as far as it goes—not talking to Celia would leave a gaping hole. He would shove us into it."

Another sigh. "Just try to wrap it up quickly, will you? Tomorrow's giving us enough headaches without having to pick apart yesterday. Remember that when you're harassing your girlfriend."

But I was already ahead of Vick, and wrapping up Frankler is what makes me slow down in the thickening traffic and peer at signs, trying without success not to think about Celia, and what kind of a meeting she's anticipating. A few hours of reminiscence, something official, or . . . something more interesting?

On the radio the DJ tells me he's busy getting the Led out, and I'm surprised that in the last three decades, ever since I played that old transistor radio in my high school bedroom, DJs haven't come up with a better way of proclaiming their love for Zeppelin. He goes on, predicting a "Beatles Block" in the next hour, and telling his listeners to call in for his "awesome two for Tuesday."

Really? Did commercial radio reach its creative peak in 1982? I switch it off.

To my left is a high school, and on the right a sign points me into the trees and down Ocean Avenue, which rolls downhill toward the coast, splitting the town of Carmel-by-the-Sea in half. The speed limit drops to twenty-five, and I ease along between two tricked-out SUVs. Carmel long ago rid itself of traffic lights, so every few blocks a four-way stop hides among the trees and cottages. I feel like I've been slipped a mild tranquilizer. It's the freshest air I've breathed in my life.

Eventually, after brief views of small homes through the trees, the shopping district appears, cut down the center by a median strip full of cultivated trees and lined on either side with cottage-themed local stores. Chains are prohibited, and the town center looks like a cinematic version of a quaint English village. Not a real English village, mind, but the kind in which Miss Marple might find herself stumbling around, discovering corpses among the antiques. I drive through the center, all the way down to the sea, passing retirement-aged shoppers dressed like golfers as they walk their little dogs, then take the sandy parking loop to get a glimpse of the clean, white beach and rough waves in the quickly fading light. There are tourists driving behind me, so I only get a moment of serenity before heading back up into the center.

I park near the corner of Lincoln and wait behind the wheel as evening descends. A smattering of locals and tourists, each one his own particular shade of white, wander the sidewalks. I'm in the middle of an idealized vision of a seaside village, rather than the real thing. An image of an image, which is a perfect place to live if you want to be something other than what you once were.

But it's nice, and I wonder if I should have reserved a room for the night instead of a seat on the red-eye back to San Francisco. I can see myself waking in this village and joining the golfers for their dawn constitutionals along the shore. The morning breeze, the sea—the kinds of things that can clean you out after a decade in the Vienna embassy. A salt wash for the soul.

After tonight, though, it'll take more than a pretty beach to scrub my soul clean, and I suspect that by the time I settle into my return flight all I'll want to do is run from Carmel-by-the-Sea as fast as my little legs can carry me.

After raising the roof with another button press and locking it into place, I take a phone out of my shoulder bag. It's a Siemens push-button I abandoned years ago for the lure of touch-screen technology. It's neither shiny nor minimalist, but it has an excellent microphone I sometimes use to record conversations inconspicuously. I power it up, check the battery, and set up the recording software. I'm the kind of person who likes a record of his life. If not for posterity, then in order to cover my ass.

Back in Vienna I used cash to refill the Siemen's pre-paid SIM, and now I dial a number I used a week ago; before that I hadn't used it in more than three years, when I made the call for Bill Compton, who was once Celia's boss. After three rings a gruff-sounding man answers. I've never seen him, so I don't have a face to imagine. I say, "Is this Treble?"

He thinks a moment. His own code name changes depending on the speaker, so in his head (or, for all I know, on an old envelope beside his phone) he goes through a list of names. Treble means that he's speaking to . . . "Hello, Piccolo. How are you?"

"We're still on?"

"A small roadster," he says. "Very feminine. In Carmel-by-the-Sea."

"Exactly."

He hesitates. "You said there were a couple mopeds and an older Chevy, right?"

"But they won't need any work."

"Yes, yes." His manner doesn't instill confidence, and I wonder how old he is. "Yes, it's all fine. I'm there."

"In Carmel?"

"Of course."

I hadn't expected him to arrive so soon.

"When do you need it, again?" he asks.

"Not immediately, but in the next few days."

"Okay, then."

"There's a chance," I say quickly, worrying about his memory, "that it won't be necessary."

"Yes, you told me this before."

"In that case, I cover travel and half your regular fee."

"I know. It's fair."

"Good. I'll call you again soon."

"Be seeing you," he says, and when he hangs up I think, *I sure as hell hope not.*

4

I arrive at Rendez-vous a half hour early, taking the existence of a bar as a hopeful omen, though I see no bottles. I'm intercepted by a young, hardly there woman in black with a ponytail atop her skull and an iPad in her hand. Even though the restaurant behind her is completely empty, she says, "Reservations?"

"Yes, but I'm early. Just getting a drink."

"Name?"

"Harrison—I mean, Favreau."

"Seven o'clock," she says approvingly to the iPad. "I can seat you now, if you like."

During the flights I sustained myself with an image of my terminal point: a stool and a long bar to support my exhausted frame. It's what I want Celia to see when she arrives—a man in a man's place. "I'll wait at the bar," I say as I slip past the waitress and, with relief, station myself at the end of the pounded-iron counter. A pert young bartender, also in black, who has sculpted his three-day beard so carefully that it looks like a layer of paint, smiles thinly. I order the gin martini I've been anticipating for the last twenty-four hours.

"Sorry. We only have wine."

"You're kidding me, right?"

He shrugs, reaching for a laminated pamphlet that lists the bottles at his disposal. It's wine country, after all. I start to read through the vineyards, but the compound names quickly blur—I don't know a thing about wine. I shut the menu. "Something very cold and strong."

"White or rosé?"

"Man, I don't care. Just make sure it's dry."

I watch him take a bottle from the fridge and waste a lot of time fooling with the opener before getting it open and pouring. He's not elegant about it, the wine glug-glugging and splattering a bit on the counter. Aware of the spectacle, he gives me an embarrassed smile. "First day on the job, sorry." Which makes me like him, just a little bit.

He slides over what proves to be a tannin-heavy Chardonnay from deep inside Carmel Valley—Joullian Estate—in a glass foggy with chill. Beside it he places a dish of macadamia nuts, then winks, still embarrassed, before heading off again. In his place a wall-length mirror gives me a full view of the restaurant.

What did I expect? Certainly not this.

It makes me think of a depressed evening a month or so ago, after returning from my final night with Linda, a new recruit from California. She was attractive and fun, smart and witty, yet at the end of the night, as I dressed and watched her smiling at me from under the sheets,

I knew that this was the end of it. So, like the man I wish I wasn't, I pretended otherwise, kissed her nose and returned to my empty apartment and began to drink heavily. I turned on the television and, flipping through the channels, stumbled upon a dramatization of a Christopher Reid poem, *The Song of Lunch*.

Sitting here waiting, I can't help seeing myself in that story of a man still stung by love, meeting his old flame for lunch at their old haunt, "Zanotti's." That poor sod imagines that time changes nothing—neither in himself nor in their restaurant. Instead, he gets the modern whitewash, a reimagined Zanotti's, not so unlike Rendez-vous, where I'm faced with

Origami ceiling aglow
like a Cubist thunderstorm,
ominous over white
reflective surfaces,
apple-green chairs
(minimalist for your discomfort),
and dustless, machine-washed
wine glasses.
Polished and peeled
monochrome wait staff
attend to every desire,
except those not
on the single-page menu.

A married couple, neither half younger than sixty, has settled at a clinically white table to read menus off another laminated card. He looks grouchy yet resigned; she has a permanent smile affixed to her face. I bet he's a cheater on the golf course, and I'll lay odds she brews an incredible iced tea.

The Siemens weighs heavily in my pocket, but I try to ignore it and focus instead on what I expect from this night.

What do I know about Celia Favreau, née Harrison? First of all, despite Vick's doubts, I do know that she's no longer mine. Five years without a word. Five years building a life in this leafy utopian outpost. Carmel, at the beginning of the twentieth century, was a temporary residence for writers and artists, who set up camp and roomed in primitive cabins along the white beach. After the San Francisco earthquake of 1906 an influx of homeless bohemians pushed the locals into finally taking city building seriously. The town's history is associated with famous writers—Upton Sinclair, Jack London, Robinson Jeffers—but I doubt those old artists would be able to afford a meal in the town it's become.

She came here to make a life with Drew Favreau, a GM manager who'd spent half his working life in Vienna before retiring at fifty-eight. They dated a mere four months, then he popped the question. The relationship confused her friends—an older man with no particularly apparent charms, while Celia's charms were apparent to everyone, particularly to the long line of young men she'd used and abandoned during her first three years in Vienna, leading up to our year together. A few years ago, Sarah Western told me that when she pressed for explanations Celia became vague and unconvincing. She wanted to stop running around, she claimed. She wanted to sit still. "A woman like her doesn't settle down," Sarah told me. "For Celia, stasis equals death."

So what was the answer? Because of our history, and because of the way I felt, I wasn't in a position to ask directly, but her friends pressed her, and their opinion finally settled on that catchall of midlife crisis. She was nearing forty, after all, her childbearing years coming to a close, and after a life in the secret world no one could blame her for wanting to rest. So, Carmel.

I haven't come unprepared—I've spent many hours on my due diligence. There is Drew, now sixty-three and a hundred and eighty pounds. There is Evan, four years old and already attending the overpriced Stevenson School around the corner from their house on Vista Street. According to school reports, it looks like Evan's shaping up to become a bully. Then there is little Ginny, one and a half, with long chestnut hair just like her mother.

There's reading to be done in a place like this, so: digital subscriptions to *The New Yorker*, *The New York Times*, the *L.A. Times*, and *The Economist*, plus a real-paper subscription to *National Geographic* (Drew's choice, I'm guessing). For a six-month period just after the move Celia maintained a Facebook page, showing off photos of the beach and quaint restaurants and upscale parties in order to feed Viennese jealousy, and it worked well—her fate was discussed throughout the embassy. Then, as if she'd done enough to make her new life convincing, she abruptly shut down the page. Old friends noticed long lags in her e-mail replies, most prefaced with "Sorry,

I've just been so busy." Over drinks, Sarah said, "We're defending the free world, right? But she's too busy to answer a lousy how-are-you e-mail?"

She *was* busy, though. She became staff photographer for the local rag, the *Carmel Pine Cone,* and volunteered at the Sunset Center, where traveling musicians, most long past their prime, came to play midcentury hits for the retirees. By the time she became pregnant the second time she had taken a part-time job at the Stevenson School, because one thing about Celia is that she knows how to lay the groundwork for her future, or her child's. She also makes time, two hours a week, to meet with Dr. Leon Sachs, her therapist, whose notes I have been unable to access.

Are all these projects enough to keep her from answering old friends? Maybe, but I don't think so. I think she decided that she was done with that existence. In Vienna she was Celia 1, and this new Celia, Celia 2, is busy jettisoning the baggage of that previous self. She's even using a therapist to make sure European phobias don't encroach on her American life. Again, she's planning ahead. She can see her quietly successful future with complete clarity, and she's cutting away anything that might threaten it.

She is, and has always been, a breathtaking woman.

5

From: Celia Favreau *<celiafavreau@yahoo.com>*
Date: October 1, 2012
To: Henry Pelham *<hpelham@state.gov>*
Subject: RE: Hey

My Dear H,

What a surprise! I thought you'd have moved on to DC by now, or to Switz—you were always crazy for those mountains. Yes, let's do meet. I've been living in a bubble of my own construction for far too long; it's time to let in some fresh air.

How's Matty? Did she fit you into a wedding ring yet? The rumors about Drew are half-true, like most rumors. He went to the emergency room with what turned out to be a heart murmur. He's on some drugs—aren't we all?—but is as fit as a 50-year-old. One that's in decent health, I mean.

The children are lovely. All children are, I suppose, but mine particularly so. Evan has begun dancing at the local academy and is at the top of his class. Ginny drew a nearly perfect face the other day—not even two yet! Obviously, both are geniuses of the highest order.

Tell Klaus to invest the security deposit into his family. That should make him happy.

Jake who?

The restaurant: Rendez-vous (yes, hyphenated—no snide comments, please), at Dolores and 6th. Let's say seven, and when we get closer we can adjust.

Looking forward to it!

Best,
C

6

The kids. The husband. Klaus. Matty, for Christ's sake. The things we talk about to avoid the only subjects that truly matter. The ways in which we distract ourselves each and every day to ignore the fact that, eventually, we will keel over and die. As if this doesn't matter, when it's the only thing that truly matters.

What I should have said in my invitation was "Celia, I can't stop seeing you when the lights go out. I see each of your parts—I atomize them—and then re-create them. They are exhibits for my own prosecution: wrists, neck, ankles. More: earlobe, chin, nipples, the cleft above your ass. For the last five years I've been defiling you periodically . . . did you know? Have you been assaulted by cold shivers around 10:00 P.M. Vienna time? That would be around one in the afternoon in California, when you're resting at home, preparing dinner for your clan, volunteering at the local theater, or taking snapshots of small business owners. Maybe you were reading *The New*

Yorker on your iPad, longing for the intellectual life of the other coast, when you felt my icy intrusion. How did it make you feel? Did it make you queasy, or was there a tickle of arousal at the base of your spine, where I once slid my hands beneath your blouse? Did that feeling stay with you through the family dinner, tugging at you as you served steamed kale and grilled chicken to your spawn, finally taking over once everyone was asleep, even that elderly man who shares the bed with you? Did you reach down to finally take hold of the feeling with your slender fingers? Could I have, just occasionally, been atomized by you? Midnight your time is nine in the morning for me. I never felt a thing, but perhaps I wasn't paying close enough attention."

My glass is empty, and I feel an urge to sneak off to the toilet. I haven't relieved myself since twenty thousand feet over Carson City, Nevada, and the mix of wine and impure thoughts brings me back to that part of my anatomy. I slide carefully off the chair and turn to find a smiling, plump woman standing beside me. Dark eyes, an angle to her head, rounded cheeks, and white gold clip-on earrings.

"I hope you're not loaded already," she says to me.

"Celia. Wow."

She laughs aloud, shaking her head. "I know I've gained, Henry, but not *that* much."

I'm confused suddenly. She's mistaking my thoughts—she's always mistaken me. "You're dreamy," I tell her and lean forward for the embrace and the kisses on the cheeks. But it's been five years, after all, and she's lost the habit. The hug is interrupted by a kiss I'm aiming at her soft left cheek, which lands instead on the corner of her lips. We separate awkwardly. "Excuse me," I mutter.

"You," she says with authority, holding me at arm's length and leaping past the faux pas. "You're exactly as you were. What's your secret?"

She lies beautifully. I've lost weight, but in the way of sickness, and the gray that once leaked stealthily into my hair staged a winning frontal assault two years ago. "Martinis," I say, "but apparently they're *verboten* here."

She puts on a frown for my benefit. "I should've chosen someplace else."

"Let's just find our table, okay?"

I watch her as we dutifully head to the ponytail. Motherhood has changed her from the long, lithe woman who crushed hearts in Austria, but love doesn't lose interest so easily. The neck. The wrists. The ankles. Those eyes and lips—fuller now, more enticing.

"Are you *leering*?" she asks, brow arched.

"Just lost in your beauty, dear."

The ponytail brings us to a table by the window via a circuitous route, and I stumble against a garishly green chair, still half-distracted by erotic memories. I'm overwhelmed by the confusion of my own incompetence. Have I really aged that much? Have I become a doddering old idiot?

Yes, probably. I mean, no. It's Celia. Here, again. Close enough to kidnap.

When I met with Bill Compton a month ago, I was on my game. I drew him to a pub of my own choosing and cut through his evasions and circumspection with a razor. By the end, he was the one distracted to the point of incompetence. His last sip of beer was delivered with a quivering hand. By the time I left, he was in a state of high panic, and not only because I brought up the Flughafen. He became a wreck because I was the polar opposite of a wreck. I was machine-made. I was in complete control of my faculties, crunching through each of his excuses with hard realities.

But with Celia? I can't imagine speaking to her that way. Not after a glass of wine and a suddenly overwhelming urge to urinate. Not still blazing from the sight of her earlobe, her shoulder-length chestnut hair, her shoulder. Christ, that shoulder.

Ponytail offers drinks, and once Celia orders a Syrah attention turns to me. What do these women want? "Henry?" Celia asks, and it takes the sound of her voice—soft, familiar, provocative—to bring me out of my funk.

I point at the bar. "Same thing I had up there. Chardonnay . . . I don't know. Ask the beard. Bartender."

Ponytail smiles and nods and withdraws.

"You must be tired," Celia says, trying not to judge. "Is the conference a bore?"

Again, I hesitate, then remember the lie: Santa Cruz. "Online encoding. Al Qaeda communication techniques. You know—JPEG of a rose turns out to be a jihadi message. That sort of thing."

"Snore."

"Precisely."

"Anyone else there? Anyone I know?"

I shake my head, not up to making the lie any more elaborate. I'm getting a feel for my limitations tonight. Outside the window it's night, the little shops subtly lit, turning slow-wandering shoppers into silhouettes. Inside, we're sharing the restaurant with only that one old couple. "Popular place?"

She follows my gaze. "Weekends, with the tourists, you can't get a table. Middle of the week, it's dependably dead." She bobs her brows. "Why I chose it."

I nod, trying to seem appreciative, then blunder into an actual conversation piece. "You must be happy here. Looks like the kind of place where it's easy to be happy."

Her head, more gently curved now, padded by the decadence of easy living, rocks. "Looks that way. I mean, it *is.* Really. Just different."

"From Vienna?"

"Of course. But from L.A. From San Francisco. From most places. People don't come here for enterprise."

"They come here after enterprise."

Two hands, wrists joined, open up beneath her chin. I'm correct—correct enough, at least.

I say, "Not boring?"

"You stay busy. Ask anyone who has kids. There's no time for boredom."

"And reflection?"

She shakes her head, smiling. "I'm not going to be cornered."

I think, *No time for noticing that chill down your spine at one in the afternoon?* I have the depressing suspicion that she would have explained it away by an oncoming cold and taken some multivitamins or ginseng root to protect herself from my molestations. Not that it would have helped. Not that anything would have.

"There's really not much to say," she goes on. "You've

seen the films. You've read the books. Parenthood's a forty-hour-a-week job with another forty hours overtime. I don't remember the last time we went out to the movies."

We, she says. It's *we* now.

Of course it's we.

"Social life?"

"Mothers meet other mothers. We discuss mothering. We obsess over our health and the health of our kids."

"So you've really done it."

"It?"

"You've left everything behind."

I can see from the lowering of her hands and the sudden lack of expression in her face that my words are not as light as I mean them to sound. Then the curtain comes down, the smile returning, and she tilts her head and stares at the high frame of the window beside us for maybe three full seconds. Then back to me. "Yes, I suppose I have. That stuff—Vienna, the Agency, the things we did there—that's not here. It's an entirely different universe."

She leaves it hanging, so I say, "And?"

"And that's the way I want it, Henry."

7

Ponytail returns with our glasses, mine sweating cold, and gives me a coy smile, almost like flirtation, but not really. It's more like pity. The bartender, I gather, has told her of my thwarted desire. I've ended up in a town that pities gin drinkers.

Celia sips her Syrah and washes it around her mouth expertly, tongue undulating to spread the manna over all her bitter and sweet buds. I try to stay away from association and largely fail. I gulp down Chardonnay like a barbarian as she says, "You didn't answer about Matty."

"No, I didn't."

"Well?"

Matty leapt into my life a week before Celia packed her bags and walked out on all of us. Austrian, twenty-six, five foot two. Energetic beyond any proven laws of physics, a manic without the required depressive periods. "She exhausted me to death."

Celia leans back, regarding me. "She *was* a bit much, wasn't she? Quite the talker."

"Scientologist, too."

This draws her back, hands on the edge of the table. "You're *kidding*."

"She was desperate to become an Operating Thetan. I ran into her a few weeks ago, and she'd made it to something called the Wall of Fire. I suppose she's communing with the aliens now."

This earns a measured laugh. "Anyone else in Henry's life?"

Sure, I think. There was Greta and Stella and Marianne and Linda, each three-night stands, each one leaving me with fantasies of a wife and mother in California. I say, "No one."

"Not a confirmed bachelor, I hope."

"Baptized, maybe."

"And the old office?" she asks, deftly swinging away from sore points.

"Vick runs it like a fiefdom. Nothing changes."

"What about Bill?"

Bill Compton was her chief during most of her time in Vienna. When she worked the street Bill received her reports, and once she moved inside he became her mentor, maybe even a father figure. "Well, he retired over a year ago. You didn't know?"

Finally, a flash of something that resembles embarrassment—something to cut through her self-satisfaction. "We haven't talked."

The relief sparkles through me, though I hide it well. I worried that Bill had called her, and the fact that he didn't makes my job here that much easier. She's unprepared.

"He lives in London now," I say.

"Sally's doing, I bet."

"Exactly. He hates it."

"She's an Anglophile bitch."

I don't know Sally well enough to reply, but the venom in Celia's voice is unexpected. Five years, and she's still angry with Bill's wife. Maybe the old life doesn't disappear so easily.

But she's changing the subject. "They still have you on the street?"

"Not for a while," I say. "I'm entirely air-conditioned now."

"Must be a nice change."

"Safer, I suppose."

"I remember quite liking the change," she says. "But I was never good at beating the pavement."

"Now you're being modest."

She shakes her head, serious.

"These days," I tell her, "I'm wasting my time with dusty files. Vick has me looking into the Flughafen disaster."

She blinks, straightens, then relaxes again before speaking. "Langley's asking?"

I shake my head and begin my lie. "Some new hotshot at Interpol is raising a stink. He thinks we have some serious soul-searching to do."

I've turned Langley into Interpol so that it won't feel quite so serious. So that she can still feel as if she's out of our reach. Yet the mere mention of the Flughafen is enough to bleed the humor out of her face. I can see this in the angle of her mouth, the crinkle at the corner of her right eye. "I'd say we did some pretty serious soul-searching back then," she says. "You remember?"

I nod.

"It was a witch-hunt."

I can't disagree with her.

"We barely got out of that with our lives, Henry, and now you're telling me some idiot from Lyon has decided to start it up again?"

"He fancies himself a historian. He's searching for inconsistencies."

"History is full of inconsistencies. How old is he?"

"Young. And yes, point taken. He hasn't outgrown his hatred of human contradictions."

"I didn't say that."

"Well, I did. But he'll learn. For the time being, it's been decided that I should give him a rococo analysis of failures and successes. A little bit of everything. And since I'm here, I might as well ask for your perspective. You mind?"

She straightens again, but doesn't relax afterward. "Is this an *interview*?"

"I'm buying you dinner, Celia. I was in Santa Cruz, and seeing you was an opportunity I didn't want to miss. I also happen to be trying to close the book on this, because I don't want anyone to open it again. None of us do. To that end, I've been talking to as many people as I can. Stuff the report full of perspectives. Be definitive. Make Interpol's head spin."

She glances across the restaurant. The old couple is

digging quietly into appetizers; the tables around us are empty. Against the corner of the bar, our waitress is chatting with the bartender. Staring in that direction, Celia says, "Did you talk to Bill?"

"Yeah, I talked to Bill. He wasn't happy about dredging it up, either."

"I don't seem happy?"

"Not really."

"Well, I am," she says, producing the broadest and least convincing smile I've ever seen. Her hands stretch across the table and squeeze the fingers of my left hand. "I've got my bestest lover here, and we're talking about things that no longer exist for me. It's like discussing dreams we've had."

"Like you do with your therapist?"

She hesitates in midbreath, rethinking whatever quick response is lying inside that deft mouth of hers. She withdraws her hands. "Have you been *investigating* me, Henry?"

"You live in California. You've seen some things. It was a shot in the dark."

Again, she hesitates. Does she believe me? Probably not. Or maybe, I think hopefully, five years in leafy bliss have dulled her senses, made her willing to believe anything that promises hope. She leans her head to the side, chestnut hair scattering against her clean neck, and says, "You haven't been here in a while, have you? Home, I mean."

"Been a few years."

"Well, it's not like it used to be. Trust me on this. These

days, people misinterpret the pursuit of happiness. They think it means the right to *be* happy. The therapists are minting money. The pharmaceuticals, too."

"Pharmaceuticals have always minted money."

"Not like now. Example. I go to see my primary doctor just after we arrive. I tell him I've got a sensitive stomach. Hell, I changed my diet completely when we came back here, so it would be a surprise if I *didn't* get some gas. He asks if I've been upset lately. Of course I've been upset, I tell him. I got married, I moved back to a country I hardly know anymore. My life is upside down. As I'm telling him this, he's writing on his prescription pad, then he rips it off and hands me a prescription for Xanax. Just like that. They give out mood enhancers like they're M&M's."

"Do they work?"

"Of course they work. I went off of them for both pregnancies, and those were the worst eighteen months of my life."

"The *worst*?"

"I'm exaggerating. We do that here. We also use the word 'love' for things we're only fond of. You have to get used to it." She raises her glass and smiles a weary one. "Welcome to California. Don't take any of us at face value."

"I'll be sure to remember that," I say, wondering if she's forgotten how well we used to lie.

8

I met Celia in 2003, after I'd transferred to Vienna. She'd landed the previous year, following a successful stint in Dublin, and had requested Vienna because it was, as she put it, "the most civilized city on the Continent." She would later change her mind about this, but the illusions of young operatives are easily forgiven.

I came from the opposite direction, limping out of Moscow with the grinding memories of the Nord-Ost siege stuck in my head. Upwards of fifty Chechen Islamic militants took over the Dubrovka Theater in late October 2002 during a performance of *Nord-Ost,* a Russian version of *Les Misérables.* Holding eight hundred and fifty hostages, they demanded the withdrawal of Russian troops from Chechnya in order to end the war that had been going on for three years. After fifty-seven hours, the Russians pumped gas into the theater and went in. Nearly all the terrorists were killed, as were a hundred and twenty-nine hostages, most as a result of the gas and the decision, inexplicable to most, not to tell treating doctors precisely what the victims had inhaled.

One American numbered among the dead—a forty-nine-year-old from Oklahoma City who'd come to meet his Russian fiancée—and in Washington and at the embassy we kept repeating his name, a kind of mantra as we joined the international condemnation of the Russian Special Forces, whose actions had led to so many unnecessary deaths. Vladimir Putin and his spokesmen raised their hands to quiet us all down and reminded us of the threat of international terrorism that, only the previous year, had felled two towers in Manhattan. Putin began sounding as much like our own president as he possibly could.

The feeling in Washington was that Russia was making an excellent point, so we relaxed our stance. Not everyone in the embassy was happy with this. My station chief, George Lito, said, "Henry, you know what's gonna happen now, don't you? If we don't raise a stink, then the Russians will dig deeper into Chechnya and keep shooting until the republic's razed to the ground." George was right: A decision to downsize Russian troops in Chechnya was quickly reversed, and a couple of weeks later new large-scale operations in Grozny and elsewhere were put into motion.

But that didn't stop us from assisting them. Under orders, we helped the FSB identify anti-Putin and pro-Chechen activists in the States, and more than once I sat down with agents to discuss dealings we'd had with Russian human rights organizations that questioned the official versions of events. Under direct orders from

George, I even gave up a Chechen source, Ilyas Shishani, who had given us privileged access into Moscow's closed Chechen community over the previous year. Soon afterward, Ilyas disappeared from the face of the earth.

Around that time in Moscow, a couple of politicians joined with a handful of journalists and former FSB officers to investigate the Dubrovka Theater disaster. Their study concluded that the FSB had used at least one agent provocateur—Khanpasha Terkibayev—to direct the terrorists to the theater. Sergei Yushenkov, a liberal politician, interviewed Terkibayev about his involvement. Soon afterward, Yushenkov was shot to death in Moscow, and Terkibayev died in a car accident in Chechnya. I was furious, but George just shrugged. "It was decided as soon as Putin made his speech. The rest of us, we're just following history." I was thin-skinned back then; I sent an angry cable to Langley to make my frustration part of the record, then requested a transfer to someplace a little quieter.

And it worked. For a while it did. After Moscow, agent management in Vienna was like a vacation, and when I met Celia Harrison in Vick's office, I was convinced I'd finally ended up in the right place. I had learned from dealing with my agents how to handle women of interest, and so I asked Celia questions about herself. She was an orphan, having lost both parents in a car accident as a teenager, and she was wise enough to know that she'd come to the CIA to replace the parental structure that had been stolen from her. Ireland had been her first foreign posting, and she'd thrived there.

When she admitted to having become a fan of rave

music while in Dublin, I insisted on taking her around to the local venues. I escorted her to Flex, the Rhiz, and the Pratersauna, and with a steady supply of mixed drinks and Advil I was able to survive the pounding noise and underaged crowds. I eventually grew to enjoy it myself. We danced—when was the last time I'd really *danced*? Celia fit so perfectly into my hands that I believed that not only had I come to a more peaceful place, I had become someone different in Vienna. For the first time in memory, I was learning to enjoy myself.

Yet she and I took time. In a handful of alcoholic slips we made out behind clubs, but she kept me at arm's length. I soon learned that while she was giving me a little of herself, she was also giving much more of herself to other men. I had to learn to set aside jealousy. I learned how not to possess a woman.

I'm still not sure how we moved from friends to lovers—whatever alchemy took place, it happened in her head. She had moved to a desk in the embassy, working under Bill, and our time together was suddenly cut in half. I pined for her, but I'd grown used to that ache. I suspect that absence really did make her heart grow fonder, for in a Turkish restaurant in Wieden she said, "I'm tired, Henry. Take me home." Only once we reached her apartment did I understand the full meaning of her words.

And there it was, precisely as I had hoped when I met her in Vick's office. We were in love, and for more than a year we made a sort of life together, piecing together hours under the cover of clandestine life in a foreign land. For once I was satisfied, which is really all anyone can ask for.

Then 2006 happened. During the two months leading to the Vienna Airport debacle, the newspapers came alive with reminders of Moscow. Two more members of the Russian investigating team that had looked into the Dubrovka Theater disaster were assassinated. Anna Politkovskaya was shot in the elevator of her Moscow apartment building. In London, Aleksandr Litvinenko was poisoned by exposure to polonium-210. My anxieties returned: the fear, the shame. I even brought up the subject to my Islamic contacts, and they shook their heads, unmoved. The tragedies that civilization faces come at an alarming rate, and dwelling on something three years old is akin to fretting about Roman history.

Maybe I should have read the signs better. Maybe the reminders of Moscow could have changed what followed. All I know is that those reminders only made me more desperate to make our relationship work. I redoubled my efforts to build a life with Celia, and in the middle of the Flughafen situation I even asked her to move in with me. By then, though, it was too little, too late.

9

Our waitress gives us an education. It's not enough to tell us that the veal is succulent; she has to explain how humanely the young cow was raised, what it ate for breakfast, lunch, and dinner, and how its brief life was cut short "in a stress-free environment." Stress, I infer, makes the veal that much less succulent. The cheese course requires a lesson in pasteurizing techniques. The vegetables give us insight into the horrors of pesticides, while the wine pairings test the limits of our considerable geography skills. The flatbread, we're told, is housemade.

"What?" I ask.

"Housemade," she repeats.

"Homemade?"

She shakes her head, the ponytail quivering at the end of her height. "No. Housemade."

Celia orders appetizers for us both and red snapper for herself. I settle on the veal. Once the waitress leaves,

Celia whispers, "They think it's European to be so fastidious."

"Really?"

"It's the only explanation I can come up with," she says, then laughs aloud, for we both know how childishly simple most European fare is. Boil for six hours, or grill for fifteen minutes, and you're done.

Then, with a smoothness that reminds me of the old Celia, she moves on to the next subject. "Are you following the campaign?"

It takes a full second to realize what campaign she's talking about. The most expensive presidential campaign in history. The first black president against the second Mormon candidate. "I'm trying not to," I admit.

"I've got no choice. Drew's volunteering. It's all he talks about."

"For which side?"

"Republican."

"Jesus."

She shakes her head. "It's hard times in America. Economy's still a mess, and either you blame Bush for breaking it, or you blame Obama for not fixing it. Everyone has his own answer. But Drew's always been a libertarian at heart, so his course is set."

"Most rich people are," I say before noticing the snide slur to my words. So I backtrack. "But don't listen to me. I'm only interested in foreign policy, and as far as I can tell Drew's guy doesn't have one."

"I'm not disagreeing," she says, her voice soft, almost coquettish. I get the feeling she's trying to tell me something more. Maybe . . . maybe nothing.

Then she starts, and I find myself getting more education. Had I known California was so educational I would've come long ago. She tells me about the various political players, both major and minor. She names campaign managers and charts donation paper trails, bemoans super PACs and the inability of the media to climb out of the straitjacket of conventional party politics. "But they're doing it to cater to their audiences. Place a liberal and a conservative in a room and watch them fight. Spectator entertainment—that's what the news has become. And the result? A stunted populace. I mean, not just the throbbing masses, but the elites as well. They've become simple." Her cheeks are pink.

Celia 2, it turns out, believes in something.

I say, "You've been paying attention."

She blinks, suddenly self-conscious. "Like I said—it's around the house all day. I don't have much choice."

Then it's gone. All the political fire, the sociological anxieties, the zealot's earnestness. Like electrons that change when observed, Celia Favreau, realizing that she's being watched, changes back into the woman who, whatever she believes, knows better than to cause waves in a town as pretty as this one. She sips her wine—nearly finished now—and says, "You didn't come here to listen to that, did you?"

"It's nice to see you fired up about something."

The pink cheeks deepen their hue. I've embarrassed her, which is a kind of victory.

Then she shakes her head. "You had questions, I mean."

"Sure, I've got questions, but that's not why I came

here, Cee. I came to see you. Find out what's going on. The other questions can wait for later."

"And what's your judgment?"

"I've got no judgment," I lie, then add a bit of truth. "I'm still collecting intel."

Another sip, and her glass is empty. A hand moves across the linen tablecloth, and with the pared nail of her index finger she lightly scratches the back of my hand.

I can't help it: For a moment I'm back in time, at the Restaurant Bauer, and even in the midst of the hell that was the Flughafen she looked so good, so put-together. I said, *You want to move in?* And she said, *In?* as a way to stall for time. As a way to maintain control. I had it all mapped out, a new stage in our lives, a way to live a little more like the people you see on the streets. A way to be human.

With her touch, my attention has slipped back down my own anatomy. I have to pee, but I don't want to lose her touch. I'll stay here until I explode.

She says, "A lack of intel never hindered your ability to judge, Henry. Tell me what you're thinking."

Stay or go? As the pressure in my bladder escalates, this is precisely what I'm thinking. Fight or flight. I turn my hand around, catching hers, and with a smile lift her knuckles to my mouth. One kiss, two. "I'll tell you everything, my dear. Just as soon as I've dealt with more pressing matters."

Which is the most elegant way I can think of to escape.

10

Urinals the world over are part of a fraternity, joined by a masculine insistence on standing while relieving oneself. Is this evolutionary? A way to remain always on guard? Or is it simple laziness? We modern humans are so disconnected from our instincts, and so connected to our leisure, that I suspect the latter as I gaze at the yellow stream noisily leaving me, last seen over Carson City.

In contrast to the spare functionality of most public bathrooms, this one has been decorated with framed photos of Greek villages, white clay structures rambling down to blue water. In one I recognize Santorini, where I vacationed disastrously with Matty, one of our last conjoined excursions. The monologues never quit, not on the shopping avenues, the beach, or the rocks we climbed, not at the table, and sadly enough not even in bed. Relaxing in the aridly beautiful Santorini landscape, touched hard by the Mediterranean sun, I found myself dreaming of Celia—Celia, who knew the limits of words, and was content to set them aside.

The rush of water is quieter than I'm used to, for this is a low-flow urinal, built to accommodate Californian water rationing—another sign of the coming apocalypse. A sign in English and Spanish tells employees precisely how to wash their hands. I read, just to be sure I've got it right, then look at myself in the dim mirror, finally seeing what she sees. It's not encouraging. Not drunk, but tired—heavy lids, bloodshot eyes, and on my chin a smear of . . . what? Oil? From where? I rub at it with some cream soap until it disappears, leaving a red blossom.

Why didn't she tell me?

When I turn to the hand-blower, something in my pocket knocks against the sink, and that's all it takes for everything to come back.

Why I am here.

Okay, maybe I'm a little buzzed as I dry my hands under the whine of the hot-air fan and then fumble with the Siemens, remembering to turn on the recorder. A red-yellow-green meter shows me the levels. "Hello," I say to it, watching the meter. "Testing." I pocket it and, gathering resolve as if I'm collecting stray rice off the floor, step back into the restaurant, nearly bumping into the ponytailed waitress as she passes with a small tray of appetizers.

I shadow her across the restaurant, sometimes stumbling to keep from running into her long, hypnotic legs, before realizing that the appetizers are for us. Her smile as I sit down seems, again, full of pity.

"I do hope you washed your hands," Celia says as I sit.

"Antibacterial, even."

"It's a question I ask every hour these days."

"Drew isn't washing his hands? I've heard that about Republicans."

She winks, giving me more credit than I deserve. "So you're going to be like that, are you?"

Our waitress has been standing patiently with her tray during the back-and-forth, and now she serves up our plates, identifying each. "For the lady, goat-cheese salad with rucola, bitter greens, and a balsamic emulsion. For the gentleman, fresh mozzarella wrapped in honey-cured, free-range bacon, with a side of rucola."

At least I'll have an excellent recording of our food.

She notices we've emptied our glasses, and we accept her invitation to drink more. As she heads off, I can't help watching those legs as they navigate around chairs. At one table, a heavy, mostly bald man with a copy of the *San Francisco Chronicle* catches her attention. He's caught mine, because I recognize him from the airport. The angry penny-pincher in the hatchback whom I don't remember from the flight itself.

"Yes, she's very pretty," says Celia. "But that's youth for you."

Embarrassed, I shake my head. "I just recognized someone."

She turns in her chair, and I see how she's pulled up her hair in the back with a tortoiseshell clip to keep those chestnut strands from contaminating her food. "From where?"

"Don't be obvious," I tell her, and she turns back, embarrassed herself.

"Sorry. A few years away, and all subtlety's gone."

"Just someone from the airport. Doesn't matter."

"Maybe it *does*," she suggests, face serious before breaking into a toothy, condescending grin. "Remember, dear. This is not the real world. You can let down your guard here."

I may be able to let down my guard, but she shouldn't.

She says, "Your bacon smells divine."

I spear a log of mozzarella and bacon and hold it out. Surprisingly, she thinks about it, as if it really requires thought. Watching her weight, perhaps. "Live a little," I tell her. I reach toward her still-so-beautiful mouth, and she gives in. She lives a little, taking it into her mouth, and as soon as her tongue touches the bacon fat her eyes close, lips purse, and she sucks everything off of the fork.

"Mmm," she says.

Indeed, it's delicious, and we both eat with pleasure, me occasionally glancing at the businessman at the far table, who reads his newspaper between sips of red. The salty pork provokes my thirst, and, just in time, our waitress brings fresh glasses.

"I shouldn't keep drinking," Celia says as I reach over to her face and, with a finger, wipe off a flake of rucola. Admirably, she doesn't flinch. She just says, "The kids still need to be tucked in."

"Can't Drew take care of it?"

She nods quickly, almost defensive. "He's amazing with the kids, actually. I sometimes think that if I disappeared, they wouldn't miss a thing. He devotes all his time to them."

"Except when he's helping the Republicans."

"Careful."

The waitress takes away our plates. I raise my glass. "To new ways of living."

This time, she hesitates. Perhaps she senses irony. Perhaps I'm buzzed enough to let my real feelings slip through the cracks between my words. I don't know. But then she smiles, and we tap glasses and drink. She sets hers down first and stares into my eyes, reading something in there. She says, "Well?"

"Well, what?"

"If you're going to ask me about Vienna, then you might as well do it before I pass out."

Involuntarily, my right hand drops to my pocket, touching the Siemens. On the other side of the room, the short-tempered businessman is digging into a plate of antipasti. Celia is waiting to be interrogated.

11

Yet as I open my mouth, running through the script, some impromptu variation on the one that brought Bill to tears, she holds up a long finger. "Don't expect a lot."

I close my mouth, look curious.

The finger moves to her skull and taps. "I don't know how much I'll remember."

"The Xanax?"

She shakes her head, still holding on to a smile. "There are collectors," she says, "and there are the other people. Jettisoners? I don't know. But I'm one of them. Remember my apartment on Salmgasse?"

"Spare."

"More than that, Henry. Empty. Every time I moved, I trimmed my life back to the basics. People do this when they're young, but unlike them I didn't have a parents' attic to slowly fill up. I didn't rent some storage facility in Queens. I just let it go, and each time I dumped old letters or photos, I felt a tingle of pleasure. *There:* One part of my history is gone. That gaggle of friends has disappeared. This collection of embarrassing memories can no longer be discovered by someone going through my stuff." She reaches for her wine, sips, thinks. "It was always about the future. What's that they say about the past?"

"That it's another country?"

She accepts my half-remembered quote. "I'm forty-five now. My kids are starting to ask questions about that other country. Their friends' parents pull out home movies and photo albums and invite aging relatives over to tell stories. What do I do? I divert their attention. Their friends are handed a long history. My kids are given nothing."

I'm not sure how to answer this. Is she talking about child rearing or the mistakes of her past? And in either case, does she expect some kind of constructive reply, or is she only showing off her anxieties so that I can admire the difficulties of parenthood? Matty was that way, her hour-long speeches uninterruptable—for if I did break in with a possible solution to her problems, I'd receive a suspicious look, followed by a fresh lecture on my inability to really *know* her.

But this is not Matty—quite the contrary. I say, "Children are resilient. I didn't get much of a history when I was growing up. You know the story." She does—abusive, alcoholic grandpa, who when he did appear at family functions was mute with eternal guilt, and whose violent history had primed the extended clan for silence. "It'll make sense when they're older. They'll be happy not to be saddled by all those connections."

"Until they have kids."

"If they have kids."

"They better," she says with the old sharpness—grandchildren are something she's already settled on. "And I better last long enough to bounce them on my knee."

I don't bother promising her anything.

She drinks more of her wine, fully now, the flesh of her throat contracting and expanding, then sets down the glass. "I'm thinking about writing a book."

I wait.

With a finger wave around her temple, she says, "Memory. This is a problem. You throw away all the evidence of your past, and you start to forget it. And it may not be pretty, but it's all I've got. So I've been taking notes. Something to leave to the kids."

"You better get that cleared."

"I'm not thinking of *publishing,* Henry. Maybe put a couple of copies in a safe deposit box, for when they come of age. Or after I'm dead. Maybe that would be better."

"Pretty sticky stuff?"

She exhales; I smell tannins and spearmint—mouthwash, or gum. "Pretty sticky."

"I'd love to read it."

"Wouldn't you just."

Arched brow, a quick lick of her lips. I gaze.

"I'm just warning you," she says. "I may get things wrong."

"You've already told me not to take you at face value, Cee."

"Did I?" A smile. "I forgot."

My expression mirrors hers as I take another gulp of wine. I say, "This should be pretty basic stuff. Chronology, mostly. I'll want you to draw me a few word-pictures. Tell me about Bill. Your responsibilities. We'll work our way up to the Flughafen."

She plants her forearms on the table, elbows together, gripping hands. Girlish excitement. "I'm all yours."

"I wish," I say, before thinking better of it. But her smile betrays nothing. "I'd like to start with your position in '06, working for Bill."

"You don't know all of that?"

"Well, you didn't tell me much, and Vick never bothered to lay it out for me. I knew better than to ask."

She pulls her arms back into her lap, considering this. Then: "You want to record our chat?"

I shake my head, then tap my temple. "I don't want Interpol asking for it later. You might say something you don't want to share."

She looks as if she appreciates my discretion; then her hand reappears, sliding forth again to grip mine. "You're looking out for me, aren't you?"

"Always," I lie.

12

EVIDENCE

Federal Bureau of Investigation

Transcript from cell phone flash card removed from premises of Karl Stein, CIA, on November 7, 2012. Investigation into actions taken by Mr. Stein on October 16, 2012, file 065-SF-4901.

CELIA FAVREAU: It is December 2006. Vienna is in the throes of Euro-phoria, a booming economy and a sense of place in the union. As always, there are anxieties—right-wingers remind everyone of Austria *über alles*, despairing the waves of immigrants from Turkey and the onetime Eastern Bloc—but by and large it's a capital of dull stability, its economy not yet shaken by the failures of Western mortgage practices.

There I am, Celia Harrison, a case officer working under William Compton, who does not enjoy being called

"Wild Bill"—a fact that stops none of us from calling him just that. An aging commander who remembers the original Wild Bill Donovan, the parachute-drop disasters in Albania and Czechoslovakia, Vietnamese humiliations, and the false dawn of perestroika. He was tired, mostly, and bent too easily by Sally's commands, to the point that none of us took his commands particularly seriously. Another way of saying that he was an excellent boss, and I'm not happy to hear he's been completely broken by his self-centered wife.

But you want positions, yes? So, Vienna station, almost entirely under diplomatic cover. Led in 2006, as now, by stalwart Victor Wallinger, chief of station, and his four disciples. Leslie MacGovern, collection management. Two operations officers: Ernst Pul, once an Austrian himself, and dear old Bill. The fourth, you'll remember, was Owen Lassiter, who ran something to do with codes. I'm not really sure what he did, but he only lasted eight months before he found himself a pistol from the storeroom, took it home, and shot himself in the head. Owen was minor American royalty, related to that Wyoming senator, which I think made him and what he did even more of a shock. We expected a prep-school jerk, but got gloomy Owen instead. Is that why Interpol's so interested?

HENRY PELHAM: Don't think so.

CELIA FAVREAU: Well, I suppose they couldn't care less.

Anyway, I'd been pulled off the street by '05, graduating from nonofficial to official, and for more than a year

I'd been working with Bill, keeping track of our networks around town, some of which I'd helped set up. We'd tapped into the Muslim community, which was by and large peaceful and hunkered down in fear, and the Russian community, which was Swiss with spies. The local gangsters helped us out on occasion, but they weren't much fun—they only helped with business issues, not the hard intel. Our real interest was in the Bundesversammlung, and over the years we'd collected enough politicians to have a pretty good insight into the shifts and turns of national policy. Enough so that Ernst came to Bill and me to find out what was going on there, rather than going to his own networks.

HENRY PELHAM: Did you like it?

CELIA FAVREAU: What?

HENRY PELHAM: Were you happy there?

CELIA FAVREAU: You remember back then—you tell me. I was busy. I was always on the move, setting up meets and grilling reluctant sources. It was the kind of career I'd always aspired to, and while there was a hint of danger the only real risk was getting kicked out of the country. I had a boss I adored. I had a civil servant's health plan. I had . . . well, I had you, didn't I? My bestest lover and a rock to lean on when I clocked out. You were still working the street, so even if I didn't have the thrill of danger I could experience it vicariously whenever I spent the night with you. I don't care what they say, Henry. A girl really can have it all.

HENRY PELHAM: Apparently not. Not you, at least.

CELIA FAVREAU: Sure, but that was later. Before the Flughafen, I wasn't thinking about the future. I was still in my thirties, and I was too busy to fret about kids. I was having the time of my life, living in a world where I could see beneath the surface of mundane reality. When Herr Fischer said something at a press conference, I was one of a handful of people who knew what he was really saying, and why. I knew which politicians had been cowed by fear or greed, and which ones had withstood those pressures. I knew who was admirable and who was not—and I knew that their public image had almost no bearing on the truth of the matter.

I knew, for instance, about Helmut Nowak. Remember him? By '05 he'd held a seat in the Bundesrat for ten years for the Greens, and suddenly he steps down. Personal reasons, he tells his constituents. The papers speculated that he was being pushed out by the new generation of Greens—the hard-core, anticapitalist wing—but they got it wrong. It was the right that was pushing him out, in particular the Freedom Party, which had evidence of a little boy he'd diddled during his years in city government. Personal reasons, indeed.

That was the high, Henry. When I heard accepted truths I was able, very often, to turn them over and read the backside, where the secrets were hidden.

I remember before Drew and I moved away, I was

talking with Sarah—Miss Western—and she was simply unable to believe that I could leave that life behind. I knew what she was getting at—most of you thought I'd gone off the deep end, or that I was marrying for money.

HENRY PELHAM: Not me.

CELIA FAVREAU: It's all right. There may even be some truth to that story. But if you flip it over you'll see the opposite. Coming over here and raising kids had always been my destination. My parents, before they died, taught me to be just like them, and they succeeded. Without the security of a family around me, I'm only half a person. It's true. The problem was that my years with the Agency were like addiction. I was drunk on the thrill of secret knowledge, too focused on the next high to ever think about what was going to make me whole. You understand? The question isn't why I moved here with Drew. The question is, Why didn't I do this ten years earlier?

13

She talks fluently and without reservation, giving voice to Celia 1, the woman who knew how to command a conversation from its start to her inevitable victory. The Celia who knew how to spin a story, invent on the fly, and draw you deep into a maze of fabrication imbued with so much authenticity that you never, not even years later, knew whether or not you had been taken for a ride.

Which makes me wonder about the differences between these two women. Are there any? Celia 1 was a professional manipulator, while Celia 2 is disarmingly earnest, which leads to the inevitable suspicion that Celia 2 is the fake here, a puppet whose strings are being caressed and manipulated by the woman who once shared my bed.

Or is it as she insists? Was Celia 2 always there, behind the constructed shell that was Celia 1? Am I finally face-to-face with the real Celia after all these years?

This, I have to admit, is a heady prospect. It calls into

question the very idea of love. Who have I been carrying around inside me all these years? Celia 1? Does that mean I've adored someone who never existed? Did I sense, in some deeper way, the other Celia hiding just beneath the surface, and fall in love with Celia 2? Or—and this is the worrisome option—did one construction allow me to more easily build the woman I wanted to love? Is my Celia, the one that has kept me up nights, just a reflection of my desires?

All this tangled self-questioning, I know, is not a sign of great wisdom, nor is it a sign of my earnestness, for I would never admit to asking the questions. Certainly not to her. Instead, it's a sign of my confusion. I'm sitting here, across from the pick that's been chipping away at my heart, and I'm not sure what to do. There is the job, the one I've flown around the world to complete—in my pocket, after all, a cell phone is recording all our words. But then there's my emotional health. It lies in my senses. I watch her speak, occasionally smell her scent, and feel the rare touch of her hand, all the while asking myself the most basic question: Do I still love this woman? Is she, as I once believed so deeply, the only person to whom I would gladly tie myself unto death? I feel, as I listen to her self-assured speech, that this is so.

Then what about the job? What about Treble, my secret weapon?

"Intelligence as drug," I say. "I like that. Vick as a pusher. Me as . . . ?"

"You're the pusher, Henry. Vick's the kingpin."

"Right. Which makes you . . . ?"

"A reformed addict," she says without a moment's

hesitation. "And I hope you're not trying to draw me back into that miserable life."

I shake my head. I might feel a breathless urge to drag her back to Vienna with me, but seeing her here, in her element, the idea grows more and more outlandish. I am, in spite of the wine, giving up my dreams. I say, "Tell me about the Flughafen."

If I want to put a damper on our conversation, this is the way. It's a subject that's avoided conscientiously in various parts of the world: Vienna, London, and Carmel-by-the-Sea. It's like bringing up the rape of a loved one in mixed company, for all of us are mixed, each having experienced the Flughafen incident in our own particular way. The subject makes some of us clam up. Others grow tense and shift quickly into anger. Bill it brought to tears.

Celia, on the other hand, leans forward. This is something new. She downs the last of her wine, and I wave to the waitress, pointing at our glasses. Celia says, "What do you want to know about the Flughafen?" Her tone is light, airy, conversational.

"How about we start with the wide-angle shot? Then we can zoom in for details."

"Everybody knows the wide-angle shot," she points out.

"Still," I say, "it's good to be sure we're on the same page."

"I thought we were always on the same page, Henry."

The waitress approaches with fresh glasses, a smile on her face. Perhaps the bartender's making clever jokes at my expense. Perhaps I'm helping him get into her pants.

Or maybe her smile has nothing to do with me, and I'm not really the center of the universe. Unlikely, but possible.

Celia lifts her glass as the waitress recedes. "To you trying to get a defenseless mother drunk."

I tap her glass with mine.

Her smart-ass toast has me dreaming again.

CELIA

1

Through his windows I can see that it's a bright, breathless morning. The kind that invigorates from the moment you open your eyes to it, the kind that gives you, if only briefly, a sticky-sweet surge of optimism. That feeling holds on, even after I've cast my eyes on the man dozing quietly beside me. A year-long mistake—that's what he felt like last night, and my last conscious thoughts before sleep were about escape, how to dislodge myself from his embrace. And now? It's like magic.

In the face of a morning like this, I forget his jealousy and his self-pity, his tender ego and his slovenly habits. In this light, Henry is a man in the encyclopedic sense, a creature of near-infinite possibility for endeavor, and for change. In those minutes before he finally opens his eyes and yawns into the back of his hand, I nearly believe that I'm an adjective I would never, at night, apply to myself: lucky.

You don't get these mornings often in the gray Austrian

winter, and you learn to appreciate them, even when you know better than to pin your hopes on the future. It's a double-edged sword. While our expectations for the future are all that really keep us going, the failure of those expectations is the source of all our sadness.

There: His eyes open. I say, "Hey." Henry says nothing, just squints at me, at the window, then with a quiet groan pulls the pillow over his head.

Expectation will get you every time.

I pad off to the kitchen and set water to boil, thinking about this. Not expectation, really, but *this:* this thing Henry and I have, now more than a year old. Sometimes it's best to begin at the beginning.

I'd arrived a year before him, so it was up to me to show him the town and introduce him to agents he would be managing. Given where he'd come from, Vick asked me to connect him with the Russian community, but after a few meetings I could see that he was troubled. The wife of a Ukrainian businessman began needling him about America's role in Putin's success, and he snapped at her: "Don't fucking accuse foreign powers of not doing what you can't do for yourself." The woman, startled, gripped her purse to her stomach, and I had to break in to calm everyone down. She eventually moved back to Kiev, but before leaving she became one of Henry's best sources.

Though I'd arrived first, it gradually became obvious that I was the junior officer when it came to working assets. I approached my agents the way I had in Dublin, with calmness and reassurance. This usually worked, but when it didn't I never blamed myself. Espionage isn't accounting; success is never assured. Henry, on the other hand, took failures personally, and despite—or because of—his emotional approach, he won more often than he lost. Agents could read his commitment in his face; they knew from his outbursts that he was human. And they responded.

No matter how much success you have with your sources, a case officer's life is still full of downtime, and Henry and I spent half our working hours in the cafés of Vienna—the Hawelka, the Museum, the Sperl, the Prückel, changing regularly for security. After exhausting work topics, we discussed things we knew better than to talk about. Where from? How here? Where to? That last one was the most difficult for me, for I had only the vaguest outline of where I was heading. Family? Sure, eventually. The States? Someday, after I've had my fill here.

Once it began in earnest, his flirtation was a marvel of clumsy seduction. I mentioned once, casually, that in Dublin I'd fallen in with the rave crowd and, despite Neanderthal doormen and tripped-out Irish youth, I'd been surprised by how much I enjoyed dancing to the blip-beeps of European house music. That was all it took for him to drag me to slick clubs all over Vienna, where I had to witness his awkward moves and try not to be embarrassed for him. Yet he wore me down, not so much by seduction as by persistence. When a man truly wants you, and is willing to hang on for months, waiting in the wings as you try out other men, you can't help but be intrigued. I even grew to appreciate his ridiculous dance moves.

The sex—beyond some groping in Austrian alleys—didn't come until I moved into the embassy and my free time came at a premium. Only with that abrupt loss of time were we able to put our few hours to better use. Or maybe it was just that, after I'd realized what a good agent-manager he was, I wanted to establish my bureaucratic superiority before letting him climb on top of me. I don't know. I just know that now, a year and three months later, I wake sometimes in his cluttered apartment on busy Florianigasse, open his refrigerator, and see it stocked with things I've added to his collection: soy milk, organic ("bio" they call it here) cheese, and eggs. I have a drawer, too—top right—with spare panties and an emergency stash of feminine hygiene products, as well as a toothbrush. Some would call this progress, but it's not. I've stored these things in his apartment for nearly a year, just as he lodges a toothbrush, a comb, underwear, and socks in my place. We've been joined in Purgatory for a long time.

Words come with coffee, me sitting on the edge of the bed, him supported by a pile of pillows. He says, "Time?"

"There's a little more. No need to hurry."

He sips, then frowns. "This isn't that soy milk, is it?"

I shake my head.

"Tastes funny."

"Arsenic," I say with a wink. "You busy today?"

He frowns at the window—he, I know, interprets the blazing sun differently than I do, because he'll be spending much of his day in its glare. It's a burden. "Vick's got me looking into some bank-related stuff."

"Bankers."

"Yeah. Right?"

A smile, finally. It's a rare thing, but when it comes it

changes the whole shape of his face, sparking little flashbacks:

Laughing at the expense of politicians in the Café Prückel.

Sharing bites of beautifully sculpted catfish and cherries swimming in vanilla custard at the Steirereck.

Necking, uncaring, in a cobblestoned alley near Fleischmarkt Straße, when the snow breaks.

In bed, his sweat-slick hand gripping my ankle as he moves his hips deeper, smiling.

The images fade as he takes his phone off the bedside table and scrolls through messages.

"You want breakfast?"

He reads the messages, eyes narrowing, and shakes his head. "Looks like I'm gonna have to go."

Which is another way of saying that I have to leave, too.

2

Though it's nearly nine when I arrive, Bill isn't in the office. He's usually in by eight thirty, which over the past year I've interpreted as his need to escape Sally's reach as soon as possible after waking. I know him, and I know her, and I carry within myself a fear of ending up in a relationship like theirs. Sally is a bully of the worst sort, for she never lays a hand on Bill, never gives her bullying a properly physical manifestation. She beats him with words and body language and selectively brutal silences. Bill, with all his Agency experience, should know better, but apparently he doesn't, and I sometimes think that I'm the one who's been given the responsibility of carrying the anger he's not strong enough to shoulder.

It may not be fair, but over the past year I've grown to truly hate Sally. Occasionally, I even broach the subject with Bill, cornering him in a subtle imitation of her aggression, so that he will sit in one place and listen. He does, but then begins to tell me stories of her history. Her mother, for instance, a glowering monster of a role model who tortured Sally all her life. Sally's first husband, Max, he of the literally backhanded rebuttals. But I remain unmoved. I am not of the childhood-trauma camp. We've all had hard times. My parents wrapped their Subaru around an electrical pole when I was fourteen. Things happen. The only thing that matters is how we deal with the now. Either we face the difficult moral decisions with ever-stronger responses, or we do not. This is what separates the mensch from the asshole. Full stop.

In my virtual in-box, among the detritus of diplomatic spam, I find a flash from Langley to Vick, duly forwarded to the rest of the staff with a request to meet in his office at nine thirty. It's from Damascus station, a terse summary of a conversation with a source they've christened TRIPWIRE.

> Source TRIPWIRE: Expect within next 72 hours an airline-related event on flight heading to Austria or Germany. Departure port uncertain—Damascus, Beirut, Amman possibilities. Group: Aslim Taslam, though the primary actors likely recruits from outside Somalia. Likelihood: HIGH.

I'm not an expert on the myriad Islamist cells that salt and pepper the planet, but Aslim Taslam has made headlines in recent years. Former members of Somalia's Al-Shabaab, they split off from the group over an ideological dispute (some reports suggested it had to do with the use of drug money to finance operations), and under their new name they approached Ansar Al-Islam, the Sunni organization formerly in Iraq, now based in Iran, for assistance. Perhaps prodded by the Iranian government, Ansar Al-Islam has given Aslim Taslam financial and logistical support, sharing networks and operational planners. With growing anxiety, Langley has watched from a distance, noting heightened cooperation between what would otherwise be antagonistic terrorist groups. In the past year, Aslim Taslam has been responsible for deaths and explosions in Rome, Nairobi, and Mogadishu. The group is on its way up.

Since Bill still hasn't arrived, at nine thirty I join the other three in Vick's large-windowed office. There's Leslie MacGovern, whose title, collection management officer, belies the fact that she's the modest brains behind Vick's rule. In her grandmother glasses, she laughs a lot, usually at Vick's jokes but sometimes at herself. She's been with him longer than any of us, and has mastered the art of feigning stupidity while passing on her real thoughts in secret. Of all of us, she's the one who excels at making Vick look good.

Ernst Pul is our naturalized spy. Born in Graz, at age ten he was brought by his academic parents to Atlanta, Georgia, a move that twisted his accent into an odd blend: down-home Austrian. He wears Swiss banker's suits and an Austrian haughtiness that three decades as a southerner haven't shaken. His peculiarities work well here, charming our opposite numbers in the Bundesamt für Verfassungsschutz, which is why he's our direct go-between with the Austrians.

Off to the side, under a black rain cloud, sits Owen Lassiter of codes and ciphers. Perpetually dismal, he blinks a lot, as if he's just visiting from a dark world of ones and zeroes, or blips and beeps, like a raver stumbling into the morning light. I'd like to like Owen—I think most of us would—but he makes it difficult.

It's not the kind of crowd I would choose on my own, and at moments like this I wish I were still on the street like Henry, who's probably drinking coffee with a source, sharing a joke and a smoke. But no—I am by nature built for four walls and central heating. Both Henry and I are where we're supposed to be.

Vick—Victor Wallinger—smiles gaudily from behind his too-clean desk. "You hear from Bill, Cee?"

I shake my head.

"Apparently Sally's taken ill."

I try to appear concerned. Leslie goes so far as to say, "Nothing serious, I hope?"

"Fainted, Bill said. Stress, maybe, but they're checking her out at the Krankenhaus. We should expect him by eleven, latest."

I nod at this, wishing Bill had phoned to warn me. Maybe, though, it really is something serious. Maybe Sally is at this moment in the throes of her final hours, and Bill is unable to see the joy that will soon be his.

"Our prayers," Ernst mutters unconvincingly, nose in a folder.

"Of course," Vick says before raising his eyebrows. "So? Aslim Taslam in our backyard. What's our take?"

Ernst is ready with an unequivocal opinion. "In Germany, maybe. But Austria? Impossible." When we look at him, waiting for more, he closes his folder. "It's a question of what they *want*. Troops out of Afghanistan?" He shakes his head and continues professorially. "The Austrians have maybe a hundred there. The Germans have the third-largest presence in the ISAF—over four thousand. Maybe they want to get some comrades out of jail? Same thing. There's only a handful of militants in Austrian prisons—which are, by the way, not unlike resorts—while Germany's holding more than its fair share. Do they want money?" Again, the head shakes. "Not these days. They don't need it, not with Tehran bankrolling them. What else?"

No one this morning seems up to standing against Ernst's unflagging self-confidence, so I say, "We're talking EU now. Not separate nations. Pick the softest target and then demand whatever you want from any of the Euro countries. You don't need to land in Frankfurt or Berlin to speak to the Germans."

Vick nods. "Good point. Ernst, you have to admit it's a good point."

Ernst shrugs, unwilling to admit anything this morning. He's sometimes like that.

Unexpectedly, Owen speaks, though he does so through the hand covering his mouth, and we have to lean forward to understand. "The online chatter suggests something broader. By necessity, TRIPWIRE is only knowledgeable about a portion of the operation. It's possible they'll use both Austria *and* Germany in a coordinated attack. It wouldn't be unprecedented."

All of us, except for Ernst, nod our appreciation of this rare event: an opinion from Owen. Vick says, "More good points. Leslie?"

She grins and waves a hand. She looks like a jolly but

eccentric aunt. "Don't ask me, Vick. Until we have something more, I'd say we're shooting in the dark."

"The ability to admit ignorance," Vick says philosophically, "is a rare and beautiful virtue."

3

The world doesn't wait for TRIPWIRE, nor does Langley, so I spend the rest of the morning finishing a lengthy report on the fallout from the Austrian legislative election back in October. The Social Democrats gained enough votes to break the ninety-two-seat majority coalition of the conservative People's Party, the nationalist Freedom Party, and the Alliance for the Future of Austria that has in various forms ruled Austria since 1999. This has left the government without a ruling coalition.

For us, there's the favorable result that Jörg Haider's Alliance has been sidelined out of governance, but now all our efforts are focused on finding out what's really going on in the negotiations between the Social Democrats and the People's Party as they struggle to put together a functioning government. We receive daily reports from agents within both parties, but the intel, I note in an aside, lacks real substance, and as a result we're unable to predict the outcome. Questions arise: Can this moment of indecision be used to our benefit? Or would an approach to President Heinz Fischer at this juncture be pointless, given Chancellor Wolfgang Schüssel's lame-duck status?

No, this is not the kind of work my lover does, and I don't think he'd be any good at it. Henry abhors the alphabet soup of Austrian political parties. To him, the ÖVP, the SPÖ, the BZÖ, and the FPÖ are all "umlaut hoarders" who are no better than B-grade movie stars. And the Greens? "Sellouts." I blame Moscow for his pessimism.

I'm about ready to send off my report when, a little before eleven, and just as Bill lumbers out of the elevator, we all receive a forwarded e-mail from Europol. I give it a quick read as I'm getting up, then give it a second look.

Bill looks as if he's been badly ironed. Gutted eyes; slack, damp lips; wrists puffy as an old alcoholic's, though he isn't one. Not yet. I follow him into his office and close the door. "Tell me, Bill."

He settles, groaning, behind his desk and runs a hand through his gray hair. "She's going to kill me, you know."

"Is she all right?"

"If you can call it that." His hands settle on the desk. "I didn't realize it at the time. Only now, driving to the embassy. It wasn't real. The heart pains, the fainting, the weeping. It's . . . well, I'm the victim of a long con. That's what I've realized. That, or an extended Pavlovian experiment. Rewards and punishment growing more intense, and now she's graduated to the next level. Before, she controlled my behavior by attacking me. Now, she's discovered how to control me by attacking herself."

I sit across from him, puzzling over this. "So she's . . . *not* sick?"

"It's a kind of sickness," he replies, then hesitates. "The human body can make itself sick at the drop of a hat. For all kinds of reasons, including revenge." He finally raises his eyes to meet mine. "I tried to leave her. Late last night. I told her I was going. Then she went on one of her rampages. At first she attacked me, and then, after she'd calmed down, there was the pain in her arm. She told me it was nothing. She told me to just go to sleep, seeing as I didn't care about her anyway. So of course I didn't sleep. I just lay there as she moaned in pain, wanting no help from me. Then this morning she went to make coffee and collapsed on the kitchen floor. Blood—she *bled* from her nose. *Christ.*"

"The doctors?"

He shakes his head. "Nothing. Nerves, maybe. Bed rest, they told her, and she's staying the night for observation."

I wonder how to answer this, but my mouth doesn't bother wondering anything. It says, "Plenty of time for you to move out your stuff. Take my apartment." I'm not even wondering if moving in with Henry is a good idea or not; I just want Bill to get away from that monster.

By the time he raises his head again, though, I know I've pushed too far and too hard. He licks some of the moisture off his lips, but it does no good. He's a wreck. "It's not that simple."

"Of course it is," I say, heedless of the part of me that knows I'm not helping the situation. "Everybody claims it's not, but it is. She's a big girl. She can take care of herself. Visit her with flowers if you like. Pay her medical bills. But her being sick doesn't make your marriage any more bearable."

A long silence follows as he stares blindly at the screen of his computer. He sniffs twice, then says, "Enough self-absorption. What's on our plate today?"

I walk him through the morning meeting, and he nods, beginning to look human again. "TRIPWIRE, you say?"

I nod.

"There was something . . ." He begins to type with determination, and I lean back, allowing him his moment of escape inside the job. He uses work that way, to sidestep the realities of his miserable life. The best of us do that. "Yes. Here. In '04 TRIPWIRE gave us a load of shit about an al Qaeda cell in Salzburg. We wasted a lot of time with the Interior Ministry, trying to get them to storm a warehouse. Empty, of course." He shakes his head. "We can keep an eye on this, but I'd say there's an eighty percent chance he's selling us another fairy tale."

"Maybe," I tell him, "but look at your in-box. From Europol."

He goes back to his computer, scrolling until he finds the message I saw when he showed up. It's a mention of the arrival of one Mashood Al-Fakeeh, on a Saudi passport, in Barcelona two days ago, arriving from Jordan. Mashood Al-Fakeeh, the analysts believe, is in fact Ilyas Shishani, a Chechen radical who reportedly joined forces with Ansar Al-Islam. It isn't much of a leap to wonder if he's one of the operational planners that Ansar Al-Islam has lent to Aslim Taslam for TRIPWIRE's "airline-related event."

Bill certainly doesn't need any prodding. He reads the message, then raises his head to look hard at me. Without a word, he nods and stands up. He's in command again, using work the way it should be used as he marches off to Vick's office.

4

Maternal feelings are the only explanation for why I insist on taking Bill to lunch when I'm not even hungry. Maternal feelings, and pity. So a little after one o'clock I tap on his door frame and ask when he last ate. He's hunched over his keyboard, gray hair scattered across his forehead. "Last night," he says, looking surprised by his own admission.

"Pack your things. I'm treating you to the Golden Dragon."

It takes some convincing, but the truth is that other than putting out an alert to watch for Ilyas Shishani and fretting about a rumor from Damascus, there's not a lot to do. He says, "You're not lunching with Mr. Right?"

"He's on the other side of town. Shaking down networks. Following leads."

"Aha," Bill says, bobbing eyebrows, then gives in. "But I'm buying."

"Yes, sir."

Goldener Drachen is nearby, down steep stairs beneath a typical Viennese monstrosity at the southern end of Liechtenstein Park and its Garden Palace. Once we get downstairs, a disarmingly cheerful man brings us into the main dining room, full of civil servants of various nationalities eating cheaply off the *Mittagsmenü,* surrounded by twisty dragons and ornate Chinese characters adorned in red. The Dragon advertises itself as Austria's first Chinese restaurant, and with its photos of famous personages over the decades, smiling with the owner, it's not hard to believe this claim.

We're in luck—a free table beside the aquarium. As we settle down Bill taps irreverently on the glass, scaring aquatic life. We ask for tea and go through the menu. Unlike the government workers around us, we're unable to bend our tastes to their preset lunch menus, and we end up ordering a smorgasbord: spring rolls, mixed grill, wonton and egg-drop soups, Hou-You chicken in oyster sauce, and Szechuan duck. Tea comes, we place our order, and once we're alone Bill returns to the aquarium and its strips of faux seaweed, through which exotic fish dart and hide. "You want to talk about it?" I ask.

I'm not sure he's heard me. His gaze doesn't shift. Then he says to the fish, "I'd rather hear about you and Henry. How is utopia?"

He wants to get his mind off of himself, and I see no reason to disappoint him. "It's complicated. Neither of us is the committing type."

He smiles, finally looking at me. "That's spooks for you. Always thinking of the angles. Protecting themselves to the point of exclusion. I'm trying to remember one example of two field agents who ended up in a successful relationship—or as successful as any relationships are these days. I can't."

This, I realize, is a significant statement. He's been in the business since I was in diapers.

"Don't take it as criticism, Cee. It's not like the rest do much better. Most couples just take longer to split up. That doesn't make what everyone else has any richer or more rewarding. Just longer."

He's failing, as anyone overcome with self-pity does. His attempt to divert himself with my romantic life simply draws him back to himself. So I offer more. "We've been at it over a year, but I sometimes feel like I don't know him any better than when we first met. Not that that's a bad thing. The mystery is still there for both of us. But that's the catch, isn't it? You start to wonder if this false sense of mystery is the only thing keeping it going."

He settles his chin on his hand and watches me with sympathy, so I go on.

"And I think—this is usually at night, when I'm depressed—that we've both become too jaded about the human race. We believe that once we get past the mystery, it'll be the same drudgery and psychic scars and childhood storm clouds that everyone has. Nothing special. Nothing worth devoting your entire life to."

"Well," he says, leaning back. "That's pretty bleak, isn't it?"

"Is it? I thought it was pragmatic. I thought I was being an adult."

A smile, then, which I realize is his first of the day, but before he can open his mouth to reply his cell phone bleeps for his attention. A full second later, mine does as well. We've received the same message, from the same source:

RED

The smile is gone now, and I suspect I won't see it again for a long while. He waves for the waiter as I go to collect our coats from the front. When I look back, he's shoveling euros into the waiter's hands, then patting him on the shoulder, receiving genial nods in reply. "They're going to deliver it," he tells me as he takes his coat from me.

Keeping a brisk pace back to Boltzmanngasse, he says, "You should allow yourself to fail."

"What?"

"People are defined less by their achievements than by the failures that brought them to where they are."

"No risk, no gain."

He shakes his head, then pauses at a streetlamp to give me his full attention. "No. No risk, no *failure*. And without failure you're not really human. You're just skating on the surface of life."

I understand him, of course, but I still feel like I need a little more. The light changes, though, and he's already walking briskly ahead. I have to jog to catch up.

5

Amman, just as TRIPWIRE said. Austria or Germany—Austria, it turns out. And, as announced in the hijackers' calls to the control tower and to ORF, the national radio and television outlet, they are indeed members of Aslim Taslam. "They've already killed a stewardess," Vick tells us. "Her name's Raniyah Haddadin."

It's a Royal Jordanian flight, number 127. An Airbus 319, which seats a hundred and thirty-eight—this day, it carries a hundred and twenty passengers and crew. Departed Amman at 10:35 A.M. and landed in Vienna at 1:25 P.M. without a hitch. According to the Austrians—based on the passenger manifest and the pilot's narrative before the cockpit was taken over—the four hijackers didn't cause any problems during the three hours and fifty minutes in the air. Then, immediately after the plane touched down, they stood up.

The first was Suleiman Wahed, a Pakistani national who sat near the rear of the plane. He unbuckled his belt and got to his feet, and when a stewardess rose and waved at him and told him to please sit, he took out a pistol and shot her in the chest. The Austrians have identified the hijackers, and have shared their names with us. Suleiman Wahed, Ibrahim Zahir (Saudi), Omar Samatar Ali (Somali), and Nadif Dalmar Guleed (Somali). We have passport photos, but not a lot more.

According to the pilot, and verified by Ibrahim Zahir's statement to the control tower, their first statement to the passengers was in Arabic and English. In essence: "Be wary, but do not be afraid. We will kill anyone who disobeys us, but we are not suicidal. We have no intention of using this plane as a weapon. We are instead using it as a safe house until our demands have been met. After that point, we will fly somewhere, and everyone will be released."

They're organized. They very quickly moved the children—nine of them, between the ages of five and twelve—into the front of the cabin to act as human shields against any forced entry, as well as leverage against anyone who wants to be a hero. "Each time someone attempts to interfere with our work," they explained to the passengers, "one of these children will die."

"That's brilliant," I admit, realizing that they've now assured themselves a docile group of hostages.

"It's inhuman," says Leslie.

Bill's hiding his face in his hands, a fresh wave of humiliation settling over him, for despite the Europol report on Ilyas Shishani's arrival in Europe, he didn't really believe TRIPWIRE's intel. Ernst, being Ernst, remains defiant, and I wonder, as I often have, just how deeply his childhood in Georgia scarred him. Was he teased mercilessly for his foreign background? Did he despise those Bible Belt children and vow to be as different from them as he possibly could? It doesn't matter, but I still wonder about it as he says with studied nonchalance, "It's unexpected, but not completely."

"No," says Vick, flashing a look at me, "because Celia already told us they might do this."

By this hour, Owen's hand has moved from his mouth to his right ear, which he tugs and manhandles until it's crimson. The nails on his fingers are just slivers, chewed as far as possible without actually biting into bone. I imagine his depression is chemical in nature, though that doesn't make me very sympathetic. I have an urge to slap that hand.

Leslie seems to be the only one without an ounce of shame. This is the benefit of advertising your ignorance.

"Demands?" Bill says to no one in particular.

Vick has it all on a single sheet of paper—an e-mail sent over from the Interior Ministry. "Five prisoners—two in Austria, three in Germany. In forty-eight hours. The Austrians tell us we've got seventeen Americans on board—we're still verifying that."

"And what's the likelihood?"

"That the Germans and Austrians will give in?" Vick scratches his nose. "There are twenty-nine Germans on board, and Angela Merkel's only been in office a few months. We don't know if that means she'll be accommodating or not, but I have a feeling she'll give in. Heinz

Fischer is a different story. The right has been beating him and the Social Democrats for being weak on immigration, and giving in would play into their hands."

"Election's done," I point out, if only because the analysis is still fresh in my mind. "The coalition negotiations aren't going to make any difference for him now. He's freer than you think."

Vick nods in my direction. "I bow to you on that, Cee. You're the expert."

I'm not, but I appreciate the deference.

Ernst says, "EKO Cobra is on standby," as if this should make us feel better. Having an Austrian assault team on standby only worries us.

Vick gives some background on Ilyas Shishani, our only real suspect outside the plane. "Chechen. Henry once knew him, and if he's in Vienna I expect Henry will be the one to find him. So he'll be spending a lot of time outdoors, sniffing around."

"Are the Austrians in the loop?" Leslie asks.

"They will be," Ernst says.

"Have the hijackers demanded fuel?" Bill asks.

Vick shakes his head, interested, then starts checking his computer for Airbus statistics. We eventually calculate about two thousand kilometers of fuel left in the tank, which doesn't leave many serious options. Among them: Tripoli. Vick promises to ask Langley to press its Libyan contacts, then raises his head to take in all of us. "We're awake, are we?"

We are.

"Good, because waiting around is not the American way. Henry's following his own leads, but we have to assume they've got other connections in town, so let's shake up our networks. Bill and Celia—that's you. Ernst, it's time to pull in favors with the Austrians. Owen. Owen—you with us?"

Owen, blinking morbidly, nods.

"I want you to talk to all our geeks around the world, but particularly in the Middle East. Comb through the chatter and tell us exactly who we're dealing with, and what they're planning next. Leslie," he goes on, turning to the ignorant one among us, "brew us up some coffee. It's going to be an all-nighter."

Leslie's head freezes in midnod. Eyes narrow.

"Kidding, Leslie. Please. I need a full sheet on each of the assholes who've taken over this plane. Find me every one of their relatives so that we can kidnap them, if feasible."

"I don't think we really need to kidnap anyone," Ernst says. "But the Austrians might want that information."

Vick shrugs. "Bring everything directly to me. Hopefully between us all we'll get some satisfaction."

The meeting breaks up, and Bill and I move to his office, calling agents and making spreadsheets of sources. We receive a call from the front desk—the Golden Dragon has delivered our lunch, and we have that sent up. I've got two women from the Muslim community to talk to, and I make appointments with each of them. Aighar Mansur can meet me in the next few hours, while Sabina Hussain pushes me off until the evening. Then I call Henry. Five rings and no answer, so I hang up, then a few minutes later he calls back. I step outside of Bill's office to answer it, saying, "You've heard."

"Of course. It's a mess."

"Maybe not so much. There's still time." I pause, remembering the open line. "We'll talk about it later."

"Dinner?"

"Maybe. My schedule's suddenly backed up. Will you be in the office?"

"Later," he says. "Probably."

"Then we'll see."

When I hang up, I find Bill looking at me through his window, almost dreamily, his mind on other things. I go back inside and ask if he's heard anything from Sally, and instead of answering he just smiles.

"What?"

"I just realized that for about an hour, I haven't thought of her." He picks up his phone. "I'll find out."

She is, of course, just fine. We finally sit down to our lunch.

6

Repeating the same procedure we used when I recruited her two years ago, I meet Aighar Mansur inside the Leopold Museum, where I find her sitting on a bench near a wall of Egon Schiele paintings, her head covered in a simple violet hijab, hands crossed on one knee. Her rationale behind this sort of meeting place lies in Islam's denial of representational art, aniconism. "No good Muslim will find himself in this temple of the body," she told me once. "We are safe."

Whether or not this is true, the fact is that Aighar has grown used to the painted presence of sentient beings, and although during our early meetings I would find her gazing awkwardly at the end of her skirt and the toes of her shoes, by now she's gathered the courage to crane her neck to take in the particulars of Schiele's fascination with the angular parts of the female anatomy.

I wonder, as I've wondered before, if this has been her desire from the beginning, this gradual descent into blasphemy, which—as she converted for marriage—is not so much a visit to someplace new as a regression into her infidel youth, when she was called Martina, and she drank and smoked dope and lived, briefly, on the streets of Vienna before finding salvation in an Iranian student's beliefs.

"It's beautiful," I say in German, settling beside her. Right now, her attention is on Schiele's *Mother and Daughter,* a woman and a girl embracing. Aighar has two daughters.

She shrugs, aware of her transgressions, and turns back to me, her voice low. "I told you, Lara, I don't know anything about it."

Lara is the name she knows me by. "I never said you did. I just wanted to find out what the community's thinking right now."

She reaches up and tugs the corners of her hijab, so as to better cover her cheeks. "What do you think? We can say, until we're blue from lack of air, that Islam is a religion of peace, but every time we start to convince someone, something like this happens. We're back to square one."

Aighar and her husband, Labib, are part of the Shia strain that was reenergized by the 1979 Iranian revolution, and because of this I tend to doubt her nonviolent claims. But I'm no expert. "What's the conversation at the mosque now?"

"You want to hear that people are taking sides? Yes, Lara. People are taking sides. Sometimes Labib says he respects hijackers like these for their unwavering faith.

It's something he respects because he doesn't share it. We all respect those who are more pure."

"Does that mean he agrees with them?"

She could choose to be insulted by that question, but she doesn't. "He praises their faith, not their actions. Their interpretation of their faith is what has gotten them into trouble."

"And the others?"

She inhales, locks onto my eyes with hers. "I could give you a list of people who are praising these men, but trust me for once: They are armchair revolutionaries. Every one of them. They offer nothing to the Islamist cause beyond a few words at the mosque and the teahouses. They aren't even praying for revolutionary successes. Do you know why? Because they're afraid. Why do you think they've moved to Vienna? Do you think they've come to establish some caliphate? No." She shakes her head. "They're terrified of sharia law. They know they wouldn't last twenty-four hours in a proper sharia state. They love our Western decadence too much."

Aighar is not a speechmaker, so all of this is a surprise. I thought I could come in here with a list of urgent questions and get my answers quickly, but something has happened to her. This is not uncommon in long-term assets. They grow weary of lies and giving their secrets to a stranger who cares nothing for them. But this feels like something different. It feels like defiance. "And you?" I ask. "Do you love our Western decadence?"

A tight grin. She looks across the room at another Schiele, *Self-Portrait with Physalis,* the artist's mottled face looking like it's in the late stages of disease. She says, "I adore it. Which is why I must leave it behind." She stands, gives me a wan smile, and adds, "But I would never allow anyone to destroy it."

Then she's gone.

It's twilight by the time I return to the embassy, and the strain is palpable. It's in the silence, everyone digging into files and making quiet calls behind cupped hands, as if by raising their voices they might draw attention to their incompetence. I'm much the same. I nod at a few faces and escape to Bill's office, which is empty, still smelling of Chinese food. Through his window I see Vick walking around the station, leaning over chairs and chatting with analysts, working to keep up morale. I have to admit, he's good at what he does. He demands and receives loyalty from his minions, and in the lofty air of his office he does an admirable job making sure our strong personalities don't clash destructively. He stops in the doorway and gives me a nod as I settle at Bill's desk. "What's the word from the street?"

"My source is being aloof, but I don't think she's hiding anything. It's the typical mixed reactions from the peanut gallery."

"Maybe we should ask the Austrians to break down some doors."

"Is that your idea, or Henry's?"

"Uncle Sam's," he says with a grin, then heads back to his own office.

There follows one of those moments when you step out of your world, just briefly, all the distractions falling away, and you see with clarity what's happening at that moment. We're sitting in our hermetically sealed embassy, making jokes about how to deal with a terrorist threat, while in an Airbus 319 parked at Vienna Airport a hundred and twenty sweating people are facing the possibility that they will die very soon. That is real; this office is not.

I pick up Bill's phone and call Henry.

"M'lady," he says.

"How are things coming?"

"Dismal. But you're looking very well."

I raise my head, and there he is, phone to ear, weaving his way between desks toward me. I hang up, and he lowers his phone as he comes in. He even steps around the desk and kisses me on the lips, fully, in full view of the embassy's CIA presence. "Well," I say.

He returns to the visitor's side of the desk and sits down, rubbing his face. He looks tired.

"Anything of interest?"

He shakes his head. "I've talked to eight people in the last four hours, and all the same. No one knows anything."

"Ilyas Shishani?"

He hesitates then, frowning. "No one's seen or heard."

"Do you believe them?"

"Sometimes you have to." He leans forward, reaching an arm across the desk toward me. The smile is back. "How about Restaurant Bauer tonight?"

We've been talking about Walter Bauer's restaurant for weeks, ever since it got a splashy write-up in the *Wiener Zeitung,* though the opportunities have slipped past us.

Usually, he's the one who doesn't have the time, but now I'm the one who says, "I don't know. I've got another meet in not too long."

"Then call me when you're done. I'll make the reservations."

As I'm mulling over the good humor in Henry's face—so out of place on a day like this, but not unwelcome—I spot Bill heading toward us, in a rush, a piece of paper flapping in his hand. He looks twenty years younger. I nod in his direction, and Henry turns to watch as Bill enters and closes the door behind himself.

"Mr. Right, Ms. Right," he says by way of greeting. "We have contact!"

7

It's a single text message, sent five hours after the hijacking began, from one Ahmed Najjar to an emergency Langley number, from which it was forwarded on to Vick.

> 4 attackers, 2 guns. Children in 1st class. Rest in econ—Muslims starboard, rest opposite. Am with Muslims, aft. Two women in critical. Water running out. No power = no cameras. Suggest rear-undercarriage attack.

"He's traveling on a Lebanese passport, but he's one of ours," Vick explains to us all, his cheeks growing pink from excitement. "A courier. Just damned good luck he ended up on the flight."

Ernst nods approvingly. "I'd say we have the upper hand."

We've each got a copy of Ahmed Najjar's file in front of us, and I've been reading through the first page. To our great relief, he is fluent in both Arabic and Farsi, but I'm not entirely optimistic. I say, "Don't be too sure, Ernst. He's had the training, but for the last six years he hasn't done much more than spike dead drops. He's also fifty-eight, working the clock until retirement. He won't be strong-arming anyone." Seeing the annoyance in his eyes, I add, "But anything's possible."

Vick's computer bleeps, and he takes a look. "He's sent one more, kids. Wait . . . *oh.*" He frowns. "Says, *Old man died of coronary. Austrian, I think.*" Vick shakes his head. "Well, that's a shame."

Ten minutes after that message, all of us, including Henry, are watching on a flat-screen television in Vick's cabinet as the door to the plane opens and an old man is lowered with rope to the tarmac. He is identified by ORF an hour later as Günter Heinz, an engineer from Bad Vöslau.

Bill asks about Ilyas Shishani. Vick says, "The Austrians are looking. We're looking. Isn't that right, Henry?"

His features stiff and serious, Henry nods. "But we're looking for a needle, and we're running out of time. Finding him is not something we can depend on." His hands move from the arm of his chair to his knees to the opposing elbows; he looks scruffy in the way only field agents do. He's the one man of action in the room, and we all know it. He says, "If we don't get in that plane soon, it's going to be a bloodbath."

"And you know this as fact," Ernst says with a hint of scorn.

"Well, it's not like the Germans are going to hand over the prisoners."

"Is this true?" Bill asks.

Vick shrugs. "We talked to the BND. They'll ship their prisoners to Vienna as a show of goodwill, but Merkel won't let them go. She thinks it's political suicide."

In the silence that follows, Henry clears his throat and forges ahead. "Ergo, we've got to get inside in . . ." He checks his wristwatch symbolically, since he's already done the math. "Well, we've got forty-two hours to crack open that can."

"There's such a thing as negotiation," Ernst explains, as if to a child. "It's what we usually start with."

I already know what Henry thinks of Ernst. ("There is no subject on which an idiot like Ernst Pul isn't an expert.") Now, he gapes at the man and says, "Negotiate? With Aslim Taslam?" He's incredulous. "Are you *kidding* me? They've already made their negotiations with Allah. Have you read their manifesto?"

Silence, for it's quickly apparent that no one in the room has any idea what he's talking about. Henry sighs loudly.

"March 2004, drafted in Tehran but sent out by e-mail from Mogadishu. It's their statement of purpose, and it lays out everything they will and will not do. For instance, they will never accept anything less than their demands. They will kill themselves before receiving anything less than their demands. This happened in Kinshasa, when the Congolese tried to negotiate. Remember?" He looks around the room—maybe we remember, maybe we don't, so he spells it out for us. "They set off an incendiary device in the central police station, burning everyone inside, including themselves. Aslim Taslam?" He shakes his head. "They do what they say, and they never go back on their word."

"Sounds like you admire them," Vick mutters.

Henry shrugs, defiant, as if he's the only one in the room who doesn't have to prove his patriotism. "They don't suffer from ambiguity. I sometimes wish we could say that about ourselves."

After a pause, Owen Lassiter says, "He's right. Either they get their prisoners, or everyone on the plane is dead. If the Germans and Austrians don't want to bow to the demands, our only option is to storm the plane before the deadline. But how do we storm the plane?"

"We?" Vick says, shaking his head. "*We're* not storming anything. We're advising the Austrians."

"How do we advise," Owen corrects, "that this be accomplished?"

"The undercarriage," Henry says. "Just like Ahmed suggested. It's been done before. Some passengers will be killed, but it's better than all of them dying."

"You're forgetting something," I say.

They look at me, Henry frowning.

"ORF. There are television cameras at the fence, watching everything. They didn't call the media on a lark—they wanted eyes on the outside of the plane."

"So the Austrians will cordon them off," Henry says.

"And what will the newscasters say?" I ask. "Will they quietly slip back? No. They'll speculate. They're desperate for fresh news, and being ordered back is the only news they'll have. It won't take a genius to speculate that the government's preparing to go in."

I feel, as their gazes return to their hands, like a wet

blanket. I check the time—I've got a meet to make. As I get up, Henry says to me, as well as to everyone else, "Then the media will need to be distracted."

The room looks at him, full of hope, but he just shakes his head. "Don't look at me. I don't know. We just need an excuse to clear everyone out."

I think he knows, just as the rest of us do, that this won't work. All we're doing now is grabbing at straws.

As I reach the door, Vick says, "Moment, Celia."

I turn.

"Keep this quiet," Vick says to all of us. "I don't want anyone—not even on the floor—knowing about our friend Ahmed."

All of us, with deference, nod.

8

My second meeting, with Sabina Hussain, turns out to be a bust. Sabina, an organizer with the Muslim Women's Foundation, calls as I wait in a depressing little café in Simmering. She's apologetic, but in her voice there's a very definite enthusiasm, for the drama at the Flughafen has brought on a rush of work for her, unnerved women seeking advice out of a fresh fear of recriminations from tough, stupid Austrian youth. "It's a zoo here," Sabina tells me, and I know she feels no regret. I wouldn't, either. Unlike conversation with me, there's nothing abstract about the faces of the desperate women she has devoted her life to helping. In a way, I envy her.

I call Henry and tell him to make those dinner reservations for now.

As I drive my embassy Ford back to the center of town, Bill calls. I put him on speaker. "Where are you?" he asks.

"Leaving a canceled meet. Heading to dinner."

"With Mr. Right?"

"Who else?"

"Listen," he says after a moment. "Our friend got in contact. Says his hosts have been talking *Russian* on the phone. What do you make of that?"

"I don't know what to make of it," I say, gliding down the Rennweg inside a constellation of brake lights. Then: "Wait. Ilyas . . ." I hesitate, trying to figure out some code for the Chechen Ilyas Shishani, but Bill's already understood.

"He speaks Russian," he says.

"Exactly."

"Which suggests?"

"That he really is in town," I answer, though we both know that it's just a suggestion, not evidence. But with his arrival in Barcelona the stars seem to be aligning. "Should I come back?"

"Have a proper dinner," he tells me. "Talk to Mr. Right about this, too. His time over there, and all."

When I find Mr. Right at the Restaurant Bauer on Sonnenfelsgasse, I'm thinking less about Ilyas Shishani than I am about fashion, because it occurs to me that my lover dresses down. I've dated more men than I care to think about, most for less time than it takes to read a menu, and by and large they were fastidious about their appearance, keeping a comb in their pocket for emergencies, shaving once or twice a day, ensuring their clothes were pressed, often by ancient local women who performed the service for pennies an item.

Henry, though, is his own kind of anomaly, the first field agent I've taken to bed. His primary duty is to blend in, to look like everyone else, which on the streets means looking disheveled. Were he to get an assignment spying in a government office, I'm convinced some untapped vanity would erupt in him, to the point of suspected homosexuality. This evening it's no different, but with the addition of a black necktie—tied correctly, I note—it's obvious he's making an effort.

He's already ordered drinks, and as he manhandles his martini, a Blauer Portugieser waits for me. He gets up and kisses my lips before helping me into my seat, all gentlemanly and suspicious. As we sit, he asks, "Progress?"

I shrug, then tell him about the most recent revelation from Ahmed Najjar. His eyebrows rise, then narrow. "Are they thinking the Russian embassy's involved?"

"Ilyas Shishani speaks Russian, doesn't he?"

He frowns, thinking about this, nodding, then says, "I never told you about him, did I?"

"Just that you'd met him in Moscow."

Moscow is not a topic we bring up often. I know of the letter he sent to Langley, disparaging the administration's reaction to the Dubrovka Theater hostage crisis, and the disillusionment that led him to flee Russia. Now a look crosses his face. It's pained, as if he's been stuck with a knife from behind, and I get the feeling we're crossing into sensitive territory.

"What is it?" I ask.

He shakes his head, waving it away, but gives me something. "I told you I was ordered to hand the FSB a list of my sources, right?"

I nod. "That's why you wrote the letter."

"It's one reason," he says, his eyes darting around the busy dining room before returning to me. "Ilyas was one of them. One of my sources. A week later I tried to make contact, but he had disappeared. No one knew what had happened to him."

"He left town?"

"Maybe, but there was no reason. His life was there, had been for at least fifteen years. He baked bread, for Christ's sake. Why would he pick up and leave?"

"You never found out?"

He shakes his head. "After I wrote my letter, they pulled me off the street. Then I came here. Later, I heard he'd ended up in Tehran. But he wasn't a radical when I knew him, and I wonder sometimes if my giving his name to the Russians pushed him over the edge."

"You blame yourself," I say, and as the words come out I realize that I like this about him. I like this nugget of self-hatred. It makes him human.

But he just shrugs.

I watch him a moment, and then the waiter arrives. He's an aging Austrian with a grandiose mustache, a throwback these days but somehow fitting in the *gemütlich* setting, and when he takes our orders—rabbit risotto with chorizo for Henry; stuffed squid with lemon and pepper sauce for me—he does so with an almost surreal level of cheerfulness. Once he's gone again, I say, "What do you think? You think he's here?"

His face settles, and for an instant I think I can see what he'll look like when he's very old. "I don't know. I'm almost ready to admit defeat."

"Doesn't sound like you."

He rocks his head from side to side.

"And that necktie doesn't look like you. What's up?"

Self-consciously, he tugs at it, then looks past me, toward the entrance. I wait. He reaches a hand across the table to hold mine. "I've been thinking."

"You know how I feel about thinking," I tell him.

He smiles. "You want to move in?"

It takes a moment to register. I leave my hand on the table, under his. It's warm. "In?"

"Well, we have choices. You can move into my place, I move into yours, or—and I think this is the better option—we get something bigger. In the Innere Stadt. Down by the river."

"You've got it all figured out."

"Well, not really," he says, leaning back and bringing his hand with him. "It's just—well, we've been at this a while now, haven't we? There's not a lot of next steps available to us."

"We could just get married," I say.

He laughs aloud at that, as if it's a joke. It is, but still. I give him a smile in return, a comforting one. He calms a little. "Well?"

Holding on to the smile, I shrug. "Let me think about it." When I see his expression, I say, "Not the answer you expected?"

He leans forward again, pushing aside the martini so he can reach both hands across the table to grip mine. "It's exactly what I expected, Cee. You're a careful girl. It's something I love about you."

But I'm not careful, and I think he knows this. I think he knows that a part of me gets a thrill from being with a field agent who sometimes comes to my house with bruises he refuses to explain, or stands me up because of "last-minute things" that, I know in my heart of hearts, he might not survive. A part of me wonders if domestication will kill what we have, while another part, which tingles down my back as he squeezes my hands, imagines the danger of cohabitation, of sudden departures in the night, of the potential for enemies to *know where I live.*

I give him a sly wink, or as sly a wink as I know how to pull off, and I wonder how it would look, that dangerous life. As we sip our drinks and play at significant silence, I wonder how far it could be pushed. First, we share the mortgage. We share towels and orange juice. We share friends and a Facebook account. We share vacation photos with family and at some point share the pedestal in a chapel, either here or back in the States, telling a small, select crowd that we're going to share our lives permanently. We send off Christmas cards, like clockwork, with shots of us sharing a shore in Martinique or Dubrovnik, and eventually we share genes, making one or two little ones whose lives we'll share unto death even if the marriage doesn't work out.

I'm jumping ahead of myself, I know, but if I've learned nothing else from the Agency, I've learned that it pays to think ahead. Eighty percent of an Agency brain is devoted to repercussions and possible futures, even when you're just thinking about moving in with your boyfriend.

I sip my wine and wonder if he's thinking the same thing.

9

We return to the embassy just in time to get shuffled back into Vick's office to listen to a message from the Austrians, relayed through Ernst: They've discovered Ilyas Shishani's lodgings, a run-down boardinghouse in Floridsdorf. Though Shishani's not there, they've gone through his few possessions and staked out the room, waiting for his return. Ernst announces this with the intonation of a high priest, as if it were something he had predicted from the outset. Sensing his self-satisfaction, Henry says, "They can sit there as long as they want. Ilyas isn't coming back."

"And you know this how, Henry?"

My lover gives him a thin smile, stands up, and begins to walk to the door. "Because Ilyas's not an idiot, Ernst."

Once we've been dismissed after a half hour of fruitless talk, I look around the office for Henry. I'm told he stepped out, and though I consider it, I decide against calling. If he wants to be alone, that's his prerogative. I'll have ample opportunity to nag when we're cohabitating.

An hour later, he still hasn't returned, and Leslie drops by to call me back to Vick's. There's been a fourth message from Ahmed Najjar. It's ten thirty.

> Scratch attack plan. They have a camera on the undercarriage. I don't know how, but it is clear they know what they're doing. Very serious. I suggest we give them what they ask for, or everyone will end up dead.

We puzzle over this. Vick says, "How the hell did they get a camera on the outside of the plane?" But we're laymen. It's like asking a sous chef to explain quantum mechanics.

Yet we try. Ernst points to Amman airport security. "I've been suspicious of them for a while. All it takes is a baggage loader to attach a camera to the hull. Operates remotely."

"But has anyone *seen* this thing?" Bill asks. "The Austrians and the TV stations have had cameras on the plane all day long—and no one noticed anything out of the ordinary?"

Leslie has come prepared, and she's attaching a laptop to the flat-screen in Vick's cabinet. Together we go over footage from throughout the day. Most of it's from ORF, but about five minutes are hi-res shots the Austrians have shared with all the concerned embassies. The quality is amazing, but I get the feeling we don't even know what we're looking for.

Unhelpfully, Owen says, "Just because we don't see it doesn't mean it's not there."

"Have we shared this last message with the Austrians?" I ask.

Vick shakes his head no.

"Then I think we'd better let them check on it. They're in a better position than we are."

My suggestion provokes a moment of hesitation. Not silence, but something tenser, and Ernst looks at Vick, who looks at Bill. Bill turns to me and, in a voice that suggests he's telling me of a loved one's passing, explains. "The Austrians don't know about Ahmed. We're trying to keep it quiet."

I feel a little stupid but recover as best I can. "Well, maybe it's time to start sharing with them. If we want to get any of those people out alive."

"The voice of cooperation," Vick says, smiling. "We're just not sure we can trust the Interior Ministry, Cee. *We* didn't vet those people."

I stare at Vick, then at Ernst. He's chewing the inside of his cheek, and I have no idea what he's thinking. I know what I'm thinking; I'm thinking that Agency paranoia has just driven us off a cliff. I take a breath, wondering how to make the obvious clear to them, but then Bill comes to my aid. "She's right," he says. "We've taken this as far as we can on our own. If we don't start trusting the Austrians this operation's going to be stillborn."

Vick rocks his head from side to side and scans the room, avoiding my eyes. "Opinions?"

Owen shrugs, then nods. Leslie just blinks rapidly. Ernst shakes his head slowly, but it's not a dismissal, for he sighs aloud and says, "Agreed."

Vick tugs at his lower lip, thinking a moment. "Ernst, make it so."

Ernst gives me a look, then takes his phone from his pocket and walks out of the office.

"Other thoughts?" Vick asks.

After a moment of hand-watching, Owen says, "It might not be him."

We raise our heads.

"Go on," says Vick.

"He may have been discovered. The only way we know that's our agent is that he's sending messages from our agent's phone."

"The code," Leslie says. "Each message is prefaced by his identifier, which is . . ." She goes through her papers, then reads it out. "Aspen3R95."

"Then it *was* him," he says, "but it's not anymore. If he forgot to delete the previous messages, then the code is on his phone for anyone to read. Or he's been forced to give them his ID—they have children on there, after all. He's discovered, maybe killed, and they took over his phone."

"But how?" I ask. Attention shifts to me. "How is he discovered? Ahmed may be just a courier, but any decent courier knows how to communicate in secret. It's what he does. How did he get caught?"

Owen shrugs. "It's just an idea."

Vick's frowning at his desktop, pulling at his lower lip.

"Pretty lousy idea. But it's a serious option, and we should keep it in mind."

"Or Ahmed's wrong," Bill says, placing a large hand on his knee. "What's his evidence? He doesn't say. He's convinced they have an external camera, but maybe he's made a mistake. It wouldn't be the first time."

"First time for him," Vick says, "or for the Agency?"

"Both." Bill straightens in his chair. "Ahmed's good, but there's a reason he's still a courier. Back in '93 he was team leader on an operation in Beirut. He thought some Palestinian gunrunners were preparing to ambush his team, so he ordered them to open fire. They were construction workers. Two killed, six hospitalized." Bill pauses for us to absorb this. "He makes mistakes."

"We all make mistakes," I say despite myself. I try to keep my disagreements with Bill to a minimum in front of the others, but I feel like I'm just stating what everyone else is thinking. "And that was thirteen years ago."

Bill shrugs, either unable to debate the point or unwilling to humiliate me in front of them—perhaps he's more loyal than I am. Either way, Vick says, "Everything's a possibility."

Everything is possible, I think, then stifle an involuntary smile. It's just hit me. Henry and I are going to move in together.

10

Bill finally leaves the office to spend some time with Sally, giving me permission to use his office for the rest of the night. When he gets into his coat and waves good-bye, I can literally see the gloom sinking into his shoulders. It's ironic that a man can stare all day long into the face of a hundred and twenty possible deaths, even be invigorated by it, while a single healthy wife can break him. Banally, I think of that old Stalin quote about tragedies and statistics, and, sitting at the desk, I can't even think of the problems in front of me. I'm wrapped up in relationships. Bill and Sally, and the miserable path they've taken. Henry and me, and our uncertain future. Is that death spiral of endless power plays in the cards for us? We are, after all, both trained in manipulation. We are both less than trustworthy.

I get coffee from the break room, mulling over this, happy to have much of the floor to myself. Gene Wilcox is dutifully processing incoming messages at his desk, and

Owen is behind his closed door, lost in a world of codes and ciphers. The others are gone, Ernst meeting with his Austrian opposite number, Vick getting a late dinner with one of his numerous girlfriends—all chosen, for security, from the embassy pool—while Leslie has run upstairs to brief the ambassador's staff. For the moment, I'm the ranking officer on the floor, but at ten before midnight that doesn't mean a whole hell of a lot.

So I return to Bill's office and go through the reports again, waiting for something to jump out at me. I think of a hundred and twenty terrified people locked on an airplane—for the hijackers, I imagine, are terrified, too. I think of Ilyas Shishani, a Chechen baker who became radicalized—maybe because of Henry's betrayal, maybe not—now running a major act of terror in Vienna. I think about Ahmed Najjar, a retirement-aged courier stuck on a sweltering plane, bravely sneaking out messages. There's a copy of Ahmed's file on Bill's desk, and I browse deeper into it. There it is—1993, the ill-fated operation in Beirut, his subsequent removal from leadership positions, and his assignment, two years later, to Pakistan to act as courier for a politically motivated general named Musharraf. This led to more jobs throughout the region, until Terry O'Reilly asked for him to be brought into the operations section permanently. There were no black marks against him after 1993, a feat that's almost suspicious.

How suspicious? Has he turned? Perhaps Ahmed boarded that plane as part of the hijacking and is being used to feed us misinformation?

It's a sign of my desperation that I even consider this. It goes against what we learned at the Farm: You go with what the evidence suggests, not with what makes an entertaining narrative. So I return to the only evidence I have: four text messages.

> 4 attackers, 2 guns. Children in 1st class. Rest in econ—Muslims starboard, rest opposite. Am with Muslims, aft. Two women in critical. Water running out. No power = no cameras. Suggest rear-undercarriage attack.

> Old man died of coronary. Austrian, I think.

> Lead hijacker on phone. Speaks Russian. Don't know enough to translate.

> Scratch attack plan. They have a camera on the undercarriage. I don't know how, but it is clear they know what they're doing. Very serious. I suggest we give them what they ask for, or everyone will end up dead.

Only with all of them in front of me do I realize what should have been obvious to each one of us sitting in Vick's office. The words, the grammar. Ahmed's earlier sentences are incomplete, telegraphed, while the fourth message contains complete sentences, the leisurely use of "it is" instead of "it's," and articles: *a* camera, *the* undercarriage.

I'm flushed, dizzy. The last message *is* from someone else.

Ergo: Ahmed has been discovered.

Involuntarily, I stand up. Then, realizing I don't know where I'm going, I sit down again and read it through once more. My impulse is to call Bill, shake him out of his marital malaise, and shout it at him. I even put a hand on his phone, but don't pick it up because the inevitable follow-up question has come to me: How? *How* was Ahmed discovered?

How is anyone discovered?

Either he made a mistake, or the hijackers received the information from the outside.

I close my eyes, remove my hand from the phone, and lay it over my forehead. If Ahmed made a mistake, we won't know about it until after the situation has ended, when witnesses tell us what happened.

If any of them survive.

Since there's no way for me to prove that Ahmed was discovered because of his own ineptitude, I have to set that theory aside and look at what's left. Namely: Someone told the hijackers about Ahmed.

Someone who spoke Russian? Ilyas Shishani?

I open my eyes, the world a little blurry, and blink until I can see through Bill's window to where Gene, our data-entry specialist, sits drinking a Coke. I look down at the messages again.

Ahmed Najjar, I know from his file, works solely for us; his name is not on any records outside of the Agency. If what Ernst told us is true—that he had not shared Ahmed's identity with the Austrians—then his identity has remained inside this office, among a small number of people. Me, Vick, Leslie, Ernst, Bill, Owen, Henry, and by necessity Gene out there.

It's not inconceivable that someone at Langley leaked the information, and it wouldn't be unprecedented, but at the moment that's not my concern. I have no way of monitoring Langley—it's beyond my reach. The only thing I can investigate is the possibility that the hijackers are getting information from someone inside this building.

Russian, I think again. Ilyas Shishani, yes, but there's only one fluent Russian speaker in the office: my Henry.

I put that away because it makes no sense. Whether or not he's the right man for me, Henry Pelham is racked by the question of rightness. He risked his career raging against our policies back in Moscow, and more than any one of us pencil-pushers he regularly risks his life for the defense of our aims. When it comes to betrayal, anything is possible, but Henry is the least likely of all possibilities.

Where to start?

For a moment, I don't know. Do I tell someone? Who? If the senior members of this station are suspects, then none of them—not even Henry—can be told anything yet. I have to start with the most basic research I can do on my own, and then work up from there. Start with embassy phone logs, in case someone was stupid enough to use an office phone. Move to cell phone records—if, in fact, I can access them without setting off alarms back at Langley. Then take another look at the personnel files, with an eye toward connections.

Keep it simple, I think.

So I get up and head over to Gene's desk among the maze of cubicles that take up most of the floor. His collar's undone, and he's bleary-eyed, already too tired to ogle me. I ask him for the phone logs.

A half hour later, after listening to Gene's patronizing refusal, then going to Sharon, Vick's secretary, for approval, I'm sitting at Bill's desk, and there it is: the line that makes my heart stop. At 9:38 P.M., a call from extension 4952. A twenty-seven-second call. To country code 962, city code 6. Jordan, Amman.

Extension 4952. Jesus.

It's unreal. A mere thirty minutes from suspicion to . . . to *this.* This is not sophisticated. It's hardly even espionage. This is child's play.

I lift Bill's phone. Then, realizing what a mistake that would be, I hang it up again and think. I have to get out of here.

I write down the number, pack up my few possessions, and put on my coat. I give Gene a distracted nod on my way out. I take the elevator and say good night to the marine on duty, who never answers with anything more than a grunt, and get one of the night staff to let me out. I walk without hesitation south down Boltzmanngasse, turn onto Strudlhofgasse, and begin to relax only once I've reached the busy foot traffic on Währinger Straße. I'm among Vienna University's science buildings now, passing students catching cigarettes in the middle of their all-nighters, when I finally spot a pay phone. It's been marked by graffiti, but it works, and I slip in a calling card.

I take a breath.

This is not where I want to be right now. I want to be at home, either mine or Henry's, in bed. Preferably with him.

Okay.

I dial the number and listen. There's the tinny *beep-beep* of a faraway phone, then a sequence of clicks before it starts to ring again, the sound a little deeper. I realize then that I've called a phone that has connected me to another line. The phone I called is a relay.

After three rings, a man answers. He says, *"Gdye Vy?"*

Though I know what it is when I hear it, I don't know Russian, and I'm not sure what to do. If I speak English, and this is Ilyas Shishani, then he will know that an American woman has his number. If I hang up, Shishani will grow suspicious. Either way, he will change his plans. So in German I say, "Luther? Is that you?"

Silence.

I can't feel my legs.

"Luther?"

Whoever he is, he hangs up.

HENRY

1

My ears tingle from the command she has of her story. The details, the fluidity. I think back a month to Bill's hesitations, contradictions, and final breakdown. I think of Gene Wilcox, the data processor who remained at his desk those forty-eight hours without a break, absorbing all the intel and pouring it into his machine. A month and a half ago I flew to Dallas to find him working for a firm called Global Security, making twice as much as he did schlepping for the government, and listened to his automaton drawl as he told me, step by step, what occurred that day. No editorializing, no detours, just the facts culled from his rather incredible memory.

"Yes, Ms. Harrison—Favreau, I suppose—was around that day. I think she arrived around nine thirty in the morning—at least, that's when I saw her. You can check the records for the exact time. She was in and out throughout the day, but when she was in the office she was usually with Mr. Compton. Now, *he* came late. That I remember. Something to do with his wife."

"But Celia."

"Yes, she was in and out. You saw her, of course. And after dinner she remained in the office for the rest of the night. Mr. Compton was gone by eleven, and she took over his office."

"Doing what, Gene?"

"I don't know. I didn't ask. Around midnight, though, she came to me. She asked for the phone logs from that day. She knew as well as I did that I couldn't do that. Any requests needed to come through Mr. Wallinger. I told her this, and she left."

"Left the building?"

"No. I assume she went to Mr. Wallinger's office, because fifteen minutes later his secretary, Sharon Lane, called asking for the same thing."

"And you sent the records on?"

"Of course. Protocol was followed."

"Did you see Celia after that?"

"She was there until nearly two in the morning. So, yes. When she left, she wished me a good evening."

"So there were no hard feelings."

A pause as he frowned at me. "Excuse me?"

"For you making her jump through hoops."

"Why would there be?"

"No reason. Was she in the office the whole time?"

"No. She stepped out once. Fifteen minutes, maybe, then she came back. She continued to work from Mr. Compton's office. And then . . . well, Ahmed Najjar. It was after that that she left the office."

Now, one and a half months later, Celia says, "It was a mess, Henry. At least, that's how I remember it. We were all off on our own tangents that day. Nothing was really unified. We met in Vick's office, but we weren't working as a single unit."

"I was running up sources," I tell her. "I didn't realize."

"Yes," she says, nodding. "You were out a lot."

Gene's favorite word comes to me. "What about protocol? Wasn't protocol keeping order?"

"You'd think so," she says. "You really would. But there was a weird disconnect that day. Ernst was calling the Austrians directly. Owen was moping over his computer. Bill was distracted by Sally. Leslie was useless." She pauses, sips her wine. "But if you want to blame someone for the chaos, talk to Vick. What does he say?"

"I haven't asked him," I tell her honestly, because while I see Vick every day there's an unspoken agreement that my Frankler investigation has nothing really to do with him. It's about me, the files, and the occasional underling who needs to be grilled for answers.

"Well, you should. You can quiz Bill and me all you want, but the buck stops with Vick."

"I did talk to Gene Wilcox."

A slender smile. "Gene? How's that little mole?" She blinks, realizing how loaded her off-the-cuff phrasing is. "I suppose he's more of a mouse."

"He's making a fortune with military contractors now."

"Good for him."

"He told me that you were looking at embassy phone records."

"Did he also tell you that he couldn't keep his hands off of me?"

I wait.

"Five times a day he performed brush passes against my ass, but he never passed me anything except his fingers. Remember how he smacked on that chewing gum?"

"Why were you looking into the phone logs?"

"Does it matter?"

"Maybe not. I'm just surprised that with everything going on you were spending time sifting through everyone's calls."

She lifts her glass, thinks better of it, then sets it back down. "Okay, Henry. I'll play. You remember what they told us at the Farm?"

"What didn't they tell us at the Farm?"

"That joker with the pirate eye patch always said, If the answer's not in front of you or behind you, remember there are four other directions to look."

"Pirate wisdom."

Thinking again, she drinks her wine, runs a tongue behind her lips, and says, "It came from Ahmed, on the plane. Do I have to walk you through all of this?"

"Just humor me."

"Okay, Henry. Ahmed Najjar was, by the grace of God, our Agency man on board. The hijackers were quick to collect everyone's phones, but Ahmed, being a good Boy Scout, had a spare one. So we received periodic messages from him. He was fluent in Arabic and Farsi, so he should have had a pretty good idea what was going on. But he didn't send us much. He told us the layout of the hostages, gave us some inside drama, and suggested an attack plan.

Then his tone changed. He was warning us off. He was telling us to cooperate."

"Because he knew they were serious."

"We *knew* they were serious. You made that clear with your little speech about their integrity. But something changed his mind."

"Like what?"

"That's the question," she says. No smile. "What made Ahmed suddenly sound like a different person?"

I wait for her to answer her own question, but she doesn't seem interested in doing this. She sips her wine and watches me coolly. I try to wait her out, but her stare is hard, almost brutal—the kind of look someone in this utopia would have no reason to master. It fills me with an odd mix of worry and arousal. Is she trying to turn the tables? Maybe, but if so she's forgotten who she's sharing a meal with. I say, "Maybe he actually was a different person."

She nods. Short, sharp.

"So you're saying he was discovered earlier than we thought?"

"It's obvious."

"Is it?"

"Yes, Henry. It was always obvious."

My lips, I notice, are dry. I lick them. "How was he discovered?"

She doesn't need to answer, and she knows it. She just watches me with those dark eyes, and it's clear now that she's waiting for me to admit defeat. I'm not ready for that. I never will be. My first step will be to show her how ridiculous she sounds.

"So it seemed reasonable to you that someone in the embassy would use an Agency telephone to call the terrorists and have a chat?"

A sigh. A long, disappointed sigh, and after facing off with her eyes that interruption is a relief. "Henry, you're an office drone now. Do you really have to ask that question?"

"I never said I was a good drone."

She shakes her head. Chestnut spreads across her shoulders. "You cover your butt," she says. "That's the first rule of office life, and if you haven't figured that out you're going to end up without a pension. If someone in the embassy is leaking information to terrorists, the very first thing you do is keep it to yourself. The second thing you do is scour the phone records, because if you don't your ineptitude is going to come out somewhere along the way. Some joker from Interpol, say, is going to point it out years later and smear your name all over the diplomatic cables."

I nod, point taken. "Did you find anything?"

"Of course not," she says. "But I was obliged to try."

She's lying, of course. This is why I've come to her doorstep.

2

It was different with Bill. An easy flight to London, where I spent a few hours taking casual surveillance of his and Sally's town house in Hampstead. Admiring that quaint, tree-lined street that led down to the Heath. Filing all the details away in order to assess exactly what kind of world he lived in now. I saw schoolchildren in their public school uniforms, bankers and financiers, some even in pinstripes, wives with the world at their touch-screen phones, and multicolored nannies pushing prams and gathering at the park to bitch about their employers in Caribbean and North African accents. I even spent twenty minutes following Sally from their home to a flower store and then to a gourmet grocer's. She looked healthy and strong in a way she had never been in Vienna, and just like with Celia I knew why: She had achieved her dream. She had emasculated her husband completely and transplanted their master-servant relationship into a country where her reins would be tightest. She had won. Her life had ended in victory.

So when I made the call from down the street, I knew that the Bill Compton I was speaking to had already been broken. I knew that all I had to do was ask the right questions.

"Henry. Well. Been a long time."

"We need to speak, Bill."

"Well, I'm sort of—"

"Now, Bill. It's urgent."

"Now? Henry, I don't—"

"*Red,* Bill. Red."

I could hear him inhale, as if he'd been sucker-punched. "Okay, Henry. Where?"

I'd found a moderately busy pub not far from him, and when we squeezed into a corner table he immediately raised his hand for a Newcastle. I ordered Coke, but when I saw the look of worry on his face, I told the waitress, "And add a little rum to it, will ya?"

He looked so damned old. An old man whose life was dictated by the whims of his wife. Whose life once represented the pinnacle of national service. Whose hands once sifted through the dirt of international affairs. Now he was a shadow of all that grandeur: a too-pale man hunched over his pint. He looked scared, and in a way I was, too. I was taking my baby steps toward freedom, and here I was faced with a man who had given up all his freedom. It was all too easy to imagine myself looking just like him one day.

I gave him the story I've given Celia. Interpol, some young upstart. But unlike with Celia, I didn't pretend it was just some bureaucratic exercise to get some foreign agency off my ass. "This analyst may be young, Bill, but he's bringing up some serious issues. And we've got to find out what's what before he does."

"All right, Henry. Happy to help. You know that."

I knew nothing of the sort, but I went on. I got him to talk about those days. He elaborated on the state of his wife's health, even admitting that he'd tried to leave her. The chest pains, the blood, the hospital. The office. As he went on, I listened coolly, wasted no effort on making him more comfortable, and watched as his anxiety increased. I slipped in suggestive questions.

"And at that moment you were *where*, exactly?"

"This is information you would have had access to, correct?"

"So with all this going on with Sally, you had a reason to be out of the office, yes?"

"You were always liberal-minded, weren't you? Sympathetic, we can say, to the economic injustices that drive groups like Aslim Taslam."

"Not as much as you," he snapped, cheeks red, sweat trickling down his cheeks. "As I remember, you adored their integrity."

I didn't need to say a thing. I just gave him a smile.

He lowered his second pint of Newcastle, eyes big. "What are you getting at, Henry? Are you trying to *accuse* me of something? What? That I was making calls to those cretins on 127? Do you know how many years of my life I've given to my country? Do you know how much abuse I've taken for my country? For the fucking Agency? They put their employees through the meat grinder. Look at me now." He opened his hands to display the worn man who looked a decade older than he should have looked. "Take a gander at your future. This is what you end up with."

I let him deliver this lecture on his martyrdom, then watched him in silence before leaning closer. "Bill, when I accuse you of collaborating with America's enemies, you'll know it. I won't be alone. There will be two big guys in the seats behind you holding on to your arms. And we won't be in a pub. We'll be in a Romanian basement. You get me? Now answer my questions before I decide to make some serious calls."

It was overkill on my part, and I knew it at the time. But you learn to spot weak points and press them hard. Bill wore his weaknesses on his sleeve. His move to England hadn't just been a capitulation to Sally—it was an escape from the traumas of life in the Agency. For the past year he had relaxed into the illusion that he had escaped as cleanly as Celia had, and when I arrived to explode that myth all his old fears and paranoia bubbled to the surface. I wondered how he had even survived to retirement.

He breathed with his mouth open, face scarlet, looking like a man being felled by a heart attack. He raised his hands in supplication. "Okay, Henry. I get it. I'm just—it still hurts, thinking about those days. Thinking about how it went to shit. I have nightmares—really. Once a week I wake up with tremors. I'm not a well man."

"Your health is another subject, Bill. Talk."

"Okay. Right. Of course we noticed the difference between Ahmed's final message and the previous ones, and we put together what that meant. We all did—we just knew better than to say it aloud. But before I left that night Vick called me in to discuss the elephant in the room."

"Just you?"

"Me and Owen. We threw around ideas. Maybe it wasn't our embassy leaking to the hijackers—if not us, then who? Iran? The fact that they were speaking Russian on the phone was a nonstarter—this was Ilyas Shishani's preferred language. But for a moment we toyed with the idea that the Russians were helping them out." He shook his head. "Helping a Chechen terrorist? No way. There were six U.K. nationals on board, so we tried to pin it on London. That made us feel better for about thirty seconds, before Owen pointed out that the U.K. embassy was staying out of the dealings—they wouldn't even know what to tell the hijackers." He took another drink. "Of course, there was always the possibility that we were wrong. Maybe this *was* Ahmed, alive and well, and he'd just decided to waste a lot of time with articles and prepositions. Or maybe it wasn't Ahmed, but he'd simply given himself away—stupidity and bad luck run international affairs as much as anything else. See?" he said, truly hoping that I could see it as he did. "We didn't know anything, not really. We were clutching at straws."

"Where was Celia?"

"Celia? She was running down contacts that didn't bear fruit. She was spending time with you. Is she still in California?"

"Did you discuss Vick's leak theory with her?"

When he shook his head again, his jowls swung like an old dog's. "Vick said to keep it locked up tight. We had to think first about controlling the fallout. So, no, I didn't breathe a word of it to her. Besides, until we really knew what was going on, she had to be considered a suspect." He hesitated, perhaps wondering if that sounded like an accusation. "Everyone was a suspect: Ernst, Leslie, you. I'm not even sure why Vick decided to trust me and Owen—it's possible he didn't, and was trying to gauge our reactions. For all I know he sat down with others for the same conversation."

"He didn't," I said.

Bill nodded at this, absorbing the news, allowing himself a moment to climb outside of his anxieties and look at everything from a distance. I could see him relaxing.

"Afterward," I said, "when those guys from Langley sat down with us, how did you explain all of it to them?"

He blinked; the tension worked its way back into his face. He reached for his beer, but it was empty. "I didn't."

"No?"

"Well, there was no point anymore, was there?"

"How's that, Bill?"

He stared at me, knowing that I was trying to provoke him but unable to do anything about it. "It was a done deal. Everything had fallen apart. If we started shouting about a mole, encouraging Langley's suspicions, then that would be the end of all of us. If you can't pin a crime on one person, it taints everybody."

"You were covering your ass."

"Exactly, Henry. And don't tell me you wouldn't do the same thing."

"I'm not the one being questioned, Bill. You're the one in the hot seat. You're the one who lied to Investigations."

"How about Vick?"

"Vick's not here right now. Owen, of course, is dead."

He opened his mouth to state the obvious, then decided against it, not wanting to make himself look any worse.

I said, "Let's go back to Celia. Why was she looking at the embassy phone logs?"

Bill leaned back, eyes narrowing. "I didn't know she did that."

"First night, after you left the office. Looked through them all."

He shook his head again, cheeks wagging. "I had no idea. Did Vick tell her to do it?"

"No, but he let her do it. What do you think she found?"

"I don't know."

"I wonder," I said, cocking my head, "what she would do if she discovered the boss she adored had placed some questionable calls from his phone. Calls to Jordan, say."

He blinked again. *"What?"*

"You see, Bill, I went through the records myself. Just a week ago. There was a direct call, from your line, to a number in Amman. About half a minute long, nine thirty-eight in the evening."

His mouth hung open, damp and stupid.

"It boggles the mind," I went on. "That someone so immersed in clandestine affairs would call from his own office phone. You said it yourself, though—stupidity runs international relations as much as anything else."

He tried to speak, but I kept going. "Took a while to trace it. I had to call in some favors from the Jordanians to get them to go through their records. The number was only in existence for a week, leading to an unoccupied studio apartment in Amman. It was disconnected two days after the Flughafen. My contacts tell me it was set up as a relay. They don't know what number it was patched to, but I can make some guesses."

His hands released the empty pint glass and settled, palms down, on the scratched tabletop. "Jesus." The color returned to his cheeks. His hands floundered. "What are you *saying*? Christ, Henry. Are you looking for a scape-goat? I never locked my office door—you know that! Anyone could have used my phone. You, Celia, Vick, Owen, Leslie, Ernst . . . are you interrogating Ernst? You should. He was the one who kept walking off to call his Austrians."

I hadn't talked to Ernst, and I had no plans to do so. My conversation with Gene two weeks earlier had shone a dim light on the technique and nuance needed to close the door on Frankler, and I didn't want to be distracted. "I'm not going to play the name game, Bill. We don't do that. We look at the evidence. We follow the evidence. Speculation is for jackasses. And this whole life you've built for yourself—your cute town house and English pubs and dinner clubs—it can disappear like that." I snapped my fingers, actually snapped them, and he flinched. "So don't fuck around with me, Bill. You don't want to end up on the wrong side of my investigation. You know we don't take prisoners anymore."

There it was: the glassy eyes. The tear forming on the red, swollen ledge of his lid. I had him. He was mine.

"Now talk to me about Celia."

3

"You really found nothing?" I ask pointedly.

She shrugs, noncommittal. "I had to check, but only an idiot would use an embassy phone."

"Yeah. An idiot." And no one would mistake Celia Favreau for an idiot. So how to explain it?

More pointedly: How to explain it without explaining it to her? How to encourage her to build the trap all by herself and then jump into it? What I need is for her to come out with it, from *A* to *Z*, in her deliciously detailed voice. *Another drink,* I think. Another drink to loosen the tongue. I lean closer and open my hands. "Let's say that someone wasn't an idiot, but they still chose to use the embassy line. How would you explain that?"

The briefest of pauses, lips pursed, brows falling. "You tell me, Henry."

"Who knows?" I shake my head, getting into the role. "We're talking about one fucked-up individual. Smart or not, the logic has to be pretty twisted."

"That's why I'd like to hear it from you, Henry."

We—both of us—are saved by Ponytail. She arrives holding aloft a tray full of California delicacies. As she serves them, announcing their names and reminding us of the education she's already bestowed upon us, I notice a hitch in her voice. The pitying smile is gone. Her hands, oddly, have lost their fluid grace, and I wonder if the bartender has been a little too forward with her back in the kitchen.

"Pan-seared red snapper with a kale and assorted fruit mélange for the lady," she announces, then swallows awkwardly as she motions to my plate. "For the gentleman, slow-roasted veal brisket in a pepper sauce with Parmesan risotto and spinach." Then, in a sudden unpredictable spasm, her left hand brushes the edge of my lip-stained wineglass. It totters and tips over. Since my reactions have already been dulled by—how many? Four? Six?—glasses of the stuff, all I can do is watch it fall. It's mostly empty, but a splash of Chardonnay splatters across my veal, leaving clear dimples in the brown sauce.

"Oh!" She leans down. "I'm *so* sorry." She picks up the glass and reaches toward my plate. "We can make up another one."

I block her movement, her buffed fingernails briefly scratching the back of my hand, and give her my most charming smile. "Don't worry about it."

Celia cranes her neck, examining the damage. "It'll go perfectly with the meat."

The waitress mutters, "But," as I hold up my hand.

"Really," I say. "No worries. I'm sure I'll love it."

Again, she hesitates, hovering beside the table until

Celia gives one of her famous smiles as she lifts her fork. "That's all. Thanks!"

As Ponytail departs, I see her look over her shoulder at me, the embarrassed horror all over her face. In the foreground, the cheapskate businessman is looking into my face, frowning with disapproval over the rim of the *San Francisco Chronicle*.

"Do they torture waitstaff in this town?" I ask.

"She's nervous from all your ogling," Celia says, sliding a bite of fish into her mouth. "Mmm. You should try this."

"I wasn't ogling," I mutter, wondering about this, then turn to find Celia holding out her fork, laden with white, flaky snapper. I taste, admit it's delicious, then cut off a forkful of pink veal. Absolutely tender, untroubled by the splash of wine. Relaxing again, I scoop up a bite for Celia, but when I hold it out she shakes her head and waves it away.

"I don't touch land animals anymore."

"How very Pacific Rim."

"You're a bigot."

"I call it as I see it," I say, then: "You enjoyed that bacon, didn't you?"

"You told me to live a little."

"Then live a little more."

She slowly shakes her fork at me, but there's no smile to accompany it. "I've lived plenty."

For a while we eat in silence, each of us transfixed by the rich blend of flavors on our plates. We were, back in Vienna, great lovers of new restaurants. Not foodies, per se, for I knew very little about what we were consuming.

We were simply able to appreciate good food, and were willing to pay for it: Zum Schwarzen Kameel, Mraz & Sohn, Kim Kocht, Steirereck . . . and the Walter Bauer, which we visited only once, during those anxious hours before the final catastrophe at the Flughafen. The same night that she would later ask Gene Wilcox for the phone logs and discover the call to Amman from her boss's phone. Why she never shared this information with Vick, or any of us, is one of the mysteries I have come here to answer.

It was a night of endings. Our last dinner out together and, some hours later, before things turned really bad on the tarmac, our final act of sex. Not the best nor the worst, but had I known then that that would be the end of our time together I would have worked harder. I would have given more and taken more. I would have committed more to memory, because afterward memories were all I had.

4

A young man with hipster sideburns approaches with wine, offering refills. He's skinny, no older than twenty-five, and on his temples are the pink scars of acne. We accept, and as he pours I say, "Is the waitress all right?"

"Sir?" he says to the glasses.

"The one who brought our food. She seemed . . . I don't know. Distraught."

He raises his eyes to meet mine, showing off a smile so wide that it strikes me as tacky. "Oh, she's all right. *Actually,*" he adds, lowering his head and his voice to a clandestine level, "she's two months pregnant. She's getting morning sickness all day long. Unpredictably. She's heading home early."

"Oh. Wish her well, then."

That garish smile. "I'll do just that." Then he's gone.

"I dream about it sometimes," says Celia, holding a

forkful of kale and fruit mélange a few inches from her mouth, frozen into a reflective pose.

"About what?"

"Flight 127. It's the stuff we don't know that gets to me—what happened *inside* the plane." She gives up on the food and settles the fork on her plate. "Their whole technique, separating the children. I certainly had nightmares about it back then, but now, with Ginny and Evan, they've become unbearable. I mean, there's nothing particularly creative about my nightmares. It's just as you'd guess. I'm on the plane with my kids, Suleiman Wahed gets up, shoots Raniyah Haddadin, then orders everyone to calm down. Then he asks for the children." She pauses again, reflecting. "What would I have done? Probably the same as everyone else. I would've held on to hope. I would have grasped at the notion that, despite all the evidence to the contrary, if I did as these men asked, everything would turn out okay. After all, even jihadis love children, right? They wouldn't hurt any of them unless they were provoked. So, like everyone else on Flight 127—except, of course, Ahmed—I would have listened carefully and followed their commands. I would not have provoked. I would not have tried to stage some coup. I would have been obedient and submissive."

I nod at this, knowing that her words are having the desired effect on me. She's asking me to put myself in the victims' shoes, to imagine their terror the way she imagines it on bad nights. But it's not necessary because she's not as special as she'd like to think. We've all had those dreams—me, Bill, Vick, Ernst, Leslie. Even Gene, I'll wager. In the last months, revisiting the files, the nightmares have been pummeling me three and four times a week.

"But in my dream," she continues, "I'm not submissive. I'm maternal. I'm angry and violent. Maybe you know, or maybe you don't, but when your kids become the center of your life, your access to violence increases tenfold. The very *idea* of someone taking them away or harming them becomes justification for any kind of violence you can imagine. Torture. Murder. Mass murder. Genocide. All these things become acceptable when your children's safety comes into question."

"Genocide?"

She shrugs. "I don't think I could give you a genocidal what-if, but maybe. Murder, though—that one is easy."

"I'll remember not to come between you and your kids."

She smiles, eyes crinkling, then picks up her fork and eats. I do the same, chewing, thinking back to the event that marked us all. With veal still on my tongue, I say, "You didn't answer my question earlier. About why a traitor would be dumb enough to use an embassy phone."

She thinks about this, and I notice her earlier reluctance has faded away. The wine, I suppose, is relaxing her, making her more confident. "I think it's obvious," she says. "Don't you?"

"Well, I'm the idiot at the table."

She shrugs again. "To undermine the Agency presence at the embassy, of course."

"Ah," I say. "That makes sense. Make the evidence blatant."

"But the question's moot, isn't it?"

I blink at her.

"Because there was no call from an embassy phone."

I nod at this lie, briefly in awe of her absolute self-control. What does she know? She knows, because I've told her, that I'm investigating the Flughafen disaster. She knows, because I've hinted at it, that I've seen the phone records. Yet look at her—the slender wrist leads to the tendons of her hand, everything perfectly still. She is at peace, entirely. Or she plays at peace perfectly. I wish, again, for a different history between us. Despite everything—despite my call to Treble and the knowledge that this is the night that will truly end everything between us—I'm swept up in mawkish romantic thoughts. How can this be?

It can be because in each man's life there are only a few women who can turn him inside out, who can cripple him with a smile. These are weaknesses, but they're also a sign of humanity. Without these flaws, a man doesn't really live.

But he can try.

When she cocks her head, examining me, I start to feel it in my stomach. A tightening, twisting, as if her look has provoked a sudden wave of bitter acid. She knows, I realize. She knows exactly what I'm up to. I'm going to have to be careful.

5

I'm finishing my food, thinking through what comes next, and when I look up I find her staring at me. She's different now, in the way a face changes with the shift of clouds over the sun. Her eyes are damp, and when I say, "Are you *crying,* Cee?" she shakes her head, wipes under her eye with the edge of her forefinger, and says, "Just thinking."

"About . . . ?"

A wan smile, then she shakes her head again. "How about you? What're you thinking?"

I think many things. I think of her ankle, and how it felt in my grip, my fingertips touching on the other side. I think of overpriced dinners and laughter. I think of waking before her occasionally and measuring out her sleeping features with my gaze. I think pitifully of years alone in my bed, desperately rebuilding her from the old schematics. I think of what I'm doing to her now, and I wonder if I'll be able to live with myself, when everything

I'm doing is in order to live. I say, "I'm thinking of our history. It's a good history."

She blinks a few times, again wiping away the tears, and straightens. She sniffs once and looks at the wine in her glass without touching it. The spell dissipates when she says, "Why don't you pin it on Owen Lassiter?"

"Excuse me?"

"He killed himself, after all. Three months after the Flughafen. No one ever explained it, not really. There was a love affair gone bad, but it went bad *after* the Flughafen." She raises her hands. "Why? Guilt destroys his relationship, then guilt and loneliness destroy him. It's a perfect little narrative, and he's not around to defend himself. Much easier than what you're doing."

She says this as if it's something that never occurred to me, though it was the very first thought that came to mind when oily little Larry Daniels approached Vick with his wicked theories. "Wouldn't work," I tell her.

"Why not?"

"Firstly, because it's not true. But that's not so important. There's a practical issue."

"Which is?"

"His family."

She raises her chin, thinking, then nods. "Right. Senator Lassiter of Wyoming."

"Two years ago, he ended up on the Homeland Security and Governmental Affairs Committee. If I pin it on his nephew, there's going to be a load of bricks falling on me. And a perfect narrative won't be enough of a defense."

"How about Ernst?"

I smile despite myself. I have a feeling she's going to

go through the whole list, just like Bill. No, not *just* like him—Bill threw out names in desperation, scratching at the dirt to keep from being smothered. There's no desperation in her voice, and it almost feels as if she's offering alternatives in order to help *me* rather than herself. Help me find another way out. Some escape route, so that I don't have to do this to her. But I've been through the options, each and every one, and this is the only avenue left to me. "The problem with Ernst is that he's still breathing."

"Aren't we all?"

Does she want me to say it? Maybe. Maybe she wants me to state the practical reason for flying to Carmel and cornering her after all these years: access. Or: *lack* of access. She is the only one of us who has built a high wall between herself and the Agency, the only one who no longer has the pull to defend herself. The irony is that the wall she built to protect herself is the very one that will trap her.

I say, "Do you want to go on with your story?"

She cocks her head, taking me in, and I get the sense that she's going to cry again. Does she really know? Does she realize that, whatever she says or doesn't say, the course has been set? I have no idea, and her reply gives me no clue. She says, "I have a theory about unhappiness. Want to hear it?"

"I'm intrigued."

She winks at me. "Don't worry—it's nothing brilliant. It's something I came up with back in Vienna, when we were together. Expectation," she says, "is the source of all human misery."

"Expectation?"

"Sure." A smile. "Like, what did I expect from California? I'll tell you: relaxation. Some luxury. A little intellectual stimulation. A safe place to mold my children. Most of all, though—the most pressing thing—was a complete escape from the Agency. I wanted to leave all of it behind. Then, about two weeks after arriving here, I get a call from a guy named Karl. With a *K.* He tells me Bill's in trouble. What can I do? I ask to know more. So he visits me at a restaurant—yes, this one—and tells me that my Bill, the one I've devoted a chunk of my life to, has turned out bad. He's been selling secrets to the highest bidder. Not to France or England or even China, but to the worst of the worst—the Islamists, the Taliban, al Qaeda. Your heroes, Aslim Taslam."

"They're not my heroes."

"Whatever. My point is that Karl wants me to help bring him down. Bill. *My* Bill. Wants me to fly to Vienna and draw him out and entrap him. The Flughafen, he tells me, is still very fresh for the Austrians. So I say to him, *Karl, are you Austrian?* He blinks a lot, wipes sweat off his brow, and says, *No, but the Austrians deserve some answers. We're going to give them answers.* What do you think of that?"

I think that it's strange that Vick never told me about this, then I think that maybe it isn't. He wouldn't have been proud of trying to pin our failures on an over-the-hill veteran just to ease relations with the Austrians. I say, "I think that's quite a story."

"Do you believe it?"

"I believe everything you say," I lie, then give her a smile to emphasize this. "What did you do?"

"I told him to go stuff himself. I told him that Bill never sold us out to the Islamists. Maybe he shared things with allies—he wouldn't be the first—but there are certain lines he would never cross."

"You really believe that?" I ask, even though I share her belief.

"I go by evidence, Henry. I go by what I know. And I'm not going to turn my life, or Bill's, upside down based on some stranger's speculation."

"Good for you. Did he accept that?"

"What could he do? He gave me his card and told me to call if I changed my mind." She shrugs, lifting her glass. "My point, dear Henry, is that the experience soured things for me here. For a long time I was disappointed in California. It wasn't as peaceful and laid back as I'd been led to believe. Not for me, at least. I became darker here, disconnected. I felt like a ghost. I told you about my visits to the doctor. I started depending on Xanax to keep me level. My life was good, but I couldn't see that. I was blind to it; I was miserable. Why? Because I'd expected too much out of this life. Had I come here expecting only a change of scenery, I would've been pleasantly surprised. But no. I had to demand everything out of my new surroundings, and I felt like I'd been cheated."

"Even with the Xanax?"

"Even with the Xanax. Until Evan. And do you know why?"

"I do not."

"Because I had no idea what to expect from him."

"Maybe I should have a kid."

She smiles at me. Neither kind nor mischievous; I can almost read pity in it. "Maybe," she says. "Or maybe not. I don't know. It's not for the faint of heart."

"Think I'm too self-centered?"

"Yes."

"Ouch."

She drinks, and I drink, and I know that she's tipsy because I'm pretty buzzed, and I've got at least twenty pounds on her. I cough into my hand and find a splash of pink spittle, a hint of blood. I clear my throat and feel the burn deep in my gut, the gases rumbling. I wonder if fine California cuisine, the kind that requires an education, is no good for me. I wonder if I've gotten too old for rich food.

"You know, Cee, I get the feeling you're trying to educate me, but I'm not sure what the subject is, or why you're doing it. Are you afraid I'm going to spread my seed somewhere? Maybe you're interviewing me to replace Drew?" She gives me a look, and I raise my hands. "Hey, a guy can dream. I'm just noting a trend in this conversation. We start with the Flughafen, and now you're steering it toward the little ones."

"Am I?" She purses her lips, as if surprised by this. "I suppose I am, aren't I? Christ, parents are such bores. Where was I?"

6

EVIDENCE

Federal Bureau of Investigation

Transcript from cell phone flash card removed from premises of Karl Stein, CIA, on November 7, 2012. Investigation into actions taken by Mr. Stein on October 16, 2012, file 065-SF-4901.

HENRY PELHAM: Ahmed's last message. You were looking into the phone records.

CELIA FAVREAU: Right. Well, it was odd, wasn't it? I mean, it wasn't just the sentiment—the idea that we should call off the attack because of some cameras attached to the outside of the plane—but it was the grammar. Completely different from before. Bill had left to go be with Sally, and I sat at his desk wondering about this.

I looked at the four messages we received, laid them out next to each other, and the difference jumped out at me. I knew it was a different person.

HENRY PELHAM: And you were right.

CELIA FAVREAU: Yes—well, maybe. Because we never found out for sure. We know he was discovered, but we don't know when he was discovered. That's a crucial point. But I had to follow through with the thought. I asked Gene for the phone records, and as he stared at my breasts instead of my eyes he refused. Since Vick wasn't in, I went to Sharon. I didn't have to explain a thing—I simply said that I wanted to take a look at the call records. She cleared it with Vick. Though he never said anything, I assume Vick suspected what I was up to. Do you know?

HENRY PELHAM: I don't know.

CELIA FAVREAU: That's strange.

HENRY PELHAM: Strange?

CELIA FAVREAU: You work with him every day. And you haven't quizzed him about all this?

HENRY PELHAM: He gives me direction.

CELIA FAVREAU: Which is another way of saying he's washing his hands of this. Putting it all on you.

HENRY PELHAM: No comment. But I do know he suspected a leak as well.

CELIA FAVREAU: Really?

HENRY PELHAM: Bill told me. [Pause.] It's not unheard of. If an administrator isn't sure if he can trust his staff, the best move is to lay low and watch everyone.

CELIA FAVREAU: Christ. I'm glad I'm not there anymore.

[Noises—glasses, drinking.]

CELIA FAVREAU: Well, Gene finally gave them to me, and I wasted an hour going through them.

HENRY PELHAM: When did you finish?

CELIA FAVREAU: One? One thirty? Something like that.

HENRY PELHAM: Then you came to my place.

CELIA FAVREAU: Yes. Well, no. First Gene and I saw the end of Ahmed on the computer. Then I came to your place.

HENRY PELHAM: And afterward?

CELIA FAVREAU: What?

HENRY PELHAM: In the morning, after I headed off, you disappeared. You have to admit it was odd. That was it for us. We'd decided to move in together, and then . . . nothing.

CELIA FAVREAU: Are you really going to do this?

HENRY PELHAM: What?

CELIA FAVREAU: Bring up *us* in the midst of an interrogation.

HENRY PELHAM: It's not an interrogation. [Pause.] Look, I'm just going through the history. You left me.

CELIA FAVREAU: I told you, Henry. I got cold feet. Standing in your kitchen while you were showering, it fell on me like a ton of bricks. You. Me. Together. Joined at the hip. Maybe not forever, but right then it felt like it would be forever. And I freaked out.

HENRY PELHAM: And within seven months you'd run off to California with Drew.

CELIA FAVREAU: Yes.

HENRY PELHAM: How does that work? A guy you've known for years terrifies you when he wants to share an apartment, but you go off and *marry* some joker you barely know?

CELIA FAVREAU: Henry. Stop. Don't ruin a pleasant meal.

[Sound of coughing.]

CELIA FAVREAU: *Hey*—are you all right?

HENRY PELHAM: [voice muffled] Shit. Just . . . I thought I was going to throw up.

CELIA FAVREAU: Here. Drink some water. [Pause.] Better?

HENRY PELHAM: Yeah. [Pause.] Anyway.

CELIA FAVREAU: You sure you're okay?

HENRY PELHAM: Yes. Go on.

CELIA FAVREAU: Okay. Well, I left your place. Then I went to the office and watched as everything crumbled.

HENRY PELHAM: What were you working on at the office? Were you making progress?

CELIA FAVREAU: I was making phone calls. Getting no answers. Listening to the noise of everyone trying to find Ilyas Shishani. You were looking for him, yes?

HENRY PELHAM: The best I did was track down another one of his safe houses, out in Penzig. But he changed places twice a day, never doubling back. He was impossible to catch.

CELIA FAVREAU: Just like you told Ernst.

HENRY PELHAM: Just like.

CELIA FAVREAU: But we did pick him up eventually, didn't we? In Afghanistan. Now he's sitting in Gitmo.

HENRY PELHAM: So you do keep in contact with the inside.

CELIA FAVREAU: Karl told me.

HENRY PELHAM: When?

CELIA FAVREAU: In June. He thought I might like to hear about it.

HENRY PELHAM: Kind of him. [Pause.] But it's old news by now, because he's since passed on to the land of forty virgins.

CELIA FAVREAU: Well. That's fortunate, isn't it?

HENRY PELHAM: Is it?

CELIA FAVREAU: [Pause.] I remember being surprised.

HENRY PELHAM: About what?

CELIA FAVREAU: You, Henry. Your background with Shishani. I was sure that you'd be the one to track him down, not some soldiers in Afghanistan. [Pause.] I sometimes wondered if he chose Vienna because of you.

HENRY PELHAM: Why would he do that?

CELIA FAVREAU: I don't know. To goad you? To try and get your help? Maybe to give himself up to you. It's just an odd thing that, of all the towns he could choose for the hijacking, he chose the one where you worked at the embassy.

HENRY PELHAM: Oh, I've thought about that, too.

CELIA FAVREAU: And? Any revelations?

HENRY PELHAM: Just that I'm not the luckiest man in the world. [Pause.] Not like Drew.

CELIA FAVREAU: [A laugh.] Henry. You sap.

7

The waiter returns to collect our plates, that garish smile still stuck to his face, and we assure him of the excellent quality of the cuisine. It's honest praise, though were I the chef I would have put a little less pepper in the sauce—my tongue is still tingling. My stomach has settled, though, and it makes me believe that there's still hope for me tonight. That I'll be able to make it through the evening in one piece and, perhaps, emerge stronger than before.

When the waiter offers more wine, Celia surprises me by saying yes for us both. Is it possible she's really enjoying her time with me, raking through the coals of a tragedy half a decade old? Is it possible (and is this the wine speaking?) that she's starting to feel the tingle of that old attraction, the easy repartee, the shared food and flesh?

When the wine and dessert menus arrive, I see that the old couple from earlier has left, and other than the businessman from the airport we're the only people dining here. He's digging into a steak, the *Chronicle* laid out on the table in front of him like a prop, and when he glances my way I wonder if it really is a prop, in the clandestine sense. This is what you get for coming to utopia with sinister motives in mind: paranoia. The man's eyes shift to take in Celia, a hint of lasciviousness there, before returning to his plate.

The waiter pours, and once he's gone Celia raises her glass. "To what?"

"To empty restaurants, the better for excellent service."

"Natch."

"What?"

She grins. "It's what the cool kids are saying. Natch—short for 'naturally.' "

"That's ridiculous."

"You need to visit home more often."

We drink.

"I really needed this," she says.

"A night out?"

"Precisely. It's been—well, it's been forever. This town is stocked with some of the best restaurants around, but we never seem to make the time."

"Children."

She sets down her glass. "Do I detect a hint of irony?"

I shake my head, trying my best to look innocent, but my innocence goes unnoticed. Her face changes slightly, darkens.

"I know what I've become, Henry. I'm a bore. But what I say is true. About kids, I mean. They change everything. You know that old cliché—I've been waiting all my life to meet you? Well, it applies to children. First as babies, but particularly once they've gotten old enough to have well-defined characters. It's completely true—you realize that you really *have* been waiting all your life to meet this person. There's nothing to compare to it."

"Not romantic love?"

She shakes her head no, then clarifies. "Apples and oranges." She takes another drink. "You think you know what love is. You've been in relationships and you've proclaimed your feelings and you've made plans for a life with someone else. But this is a different animal. There's no ego getting in the way. It's evolutionary. It's . . ." She hesitates, searching for the word. "It's *complete.* Beside it, romantic love is cute. Passion is just a little game. Aspirations for yourself—those, too. *Everything* is darkened by the shadow of your love for your child."

I smile at her, and my stomach hurts again. My eyes are watery, and I reach for the wine to cover up my consternation. Because now I get it. I understand the lesson plan she's been laying out for me. She's teaching me something so advanced that she has to spell it out for me with the clarity and simplicity of *Dick and Jane.* She's teaching me that what we had, and what we lost, means nothing to her, and it hasn't meant anything to her for years. She was incomplete with me; without me, she's finally whole.

I don't know what to say. The infantile, lovelorn part of me wants specificity, wants to press her: *Are you really saying that what we had means* nothing *to you?* But that same part is terrified of the answer. If she verifies my fear, then I'll know that the choices I made, the very ones that have *defined* me for years, were not only reprehensible but senseless.

If she tells me otherwise, she'll be lying, and I'll know it.

"Well," I say finally. "You've convinced me."

"Of what?"

I look past her, then tug unconsciously at the tip of my nose. "That I really need to go to the bathroom." I get up, but too quickly, and the blood rushes to my head. I swoon.

"You okay?"

I'm dizzy and I'm ill, but I don't want her sympathy. My face, I can feel, is red. "Be right back," I mutter, and stumble off.

8

With my forehead against the tile wall beside that view of Santorini, I watch with moderate surprise as my clear stream turns pink. I let out an involuntary "Oh!" before remembering the phone. I take it out and find that it's still diligently recording everything—forty-six minutes' worth of conversation, and a man urinating. I pause it, pocket it, and stare with fascination at the last of the pink urine disappearing. I don't even look up as I hear the bathroom door open and close behind me. I'm wondering what my liver's doing now. I've been a heavy drinker for far too long, and now, I suppose, my organs are starting to rebel.

Beside me, the businessman unzips his fly and pulls out his member. I straighten up, woozy. The man says, "You all right?"

I nod, zip myself up, and walk carefully over to the sinks. The man says something I don't hear over the rush of the faucet. I splash cold water on my sweaty face. Then he appears beside me and repeats himself, "I said, *Is everything going to plan, Piccolo?*"

I look at him in the mirror. Heavy, just as I remember from the airport, with a few days' beard on his cheeks. Tired-looking, as if he's been traveling a long time. "Treble?"

He smiles, nodding.

"What are you doing here?"

"Scouting the territory," he says as he dispenses soft soap into his hand and massages it in. Then he raises a soapy finger. "Oh! You mean, how did I *know* who you were? Isn't that what you meant?"

I nod, feeling utterly stupid.

"You used the old phone," he says. "In the old days you called for Bill Compton, and it was just a matter of putting it together."

"I'm not the only one who called for Bill Compton."

"Sure," he says, "but I started watching incoming flights. I saw you arrive."

The stupid agent puts it together, finally. "You weren't on my plane."

"Thought it was a good time to change cars, but I've been here for days. She lives over on Junipero and Vista. Hey, did you realize that most of this town doesn't even have street addresses? Crazy. No mail delivery, and if you want a pizza delivered you have to tell them the street corner, and how many houses north or south of it. Weird place. They almost didn't let me come in. In the restaurant, I mean. Guess I'm not dressed well enough."

I look at his open-collared shirt, his wrinkled jacket

and baggy pants. He doesn't look so bad to me, but my standards are tragically low.

He says, "You were in here. The waitress tried to tell me they were expecting a large party, so I had to make a scene. Eventually, the bartender came over and told her I could stay." He sniffs, then wipes his nose with a thumb. "Snobs."

"Yeah," I say, then turn off the water and dry my hands with some towels folded in a perfect tower beside the sink. "Look, I didn't expect to run into you."

"Everyone has his technique," he says, smiling. "I shadow first."

"Right," I say, but that's not what I'm thinking. I'm thinking, *You don't look right.* But what is right? Men like these, you never see. All you see is the results of their visits. So, without anything to go by, we tend to cast them from fiction. Matt Damon, Jean-Claude Van Damme, Jean Reno. Not a guy who looks like an overfed Willy Loman, or like my father's depressed drinking buddies who watched the games on our TV as Dad burned dogs on the grill, the friends who passed around Lee Iacocca's autobiography as if it were a map to a treasure that had eluded them all.

No—Treble is not supposed to look like this.

"So?" he says, closing the tap. "Are we still on?"

I chew my lower lip, thinking about it. "I don't know."

He claps a hand on my shoulder. "And if it's called off?"

"Half your fee."

"Plus travel." He winks and walks out of the bathroom. I stare at myself in the mirror for a full minute, thinking about Treble and code names and cell phones and Celia, about her new religion, the one rooted in the upbringing of children. From international intrigue to diapers. From governmental secrets to Barney. From dangerous streets to private-school admissions. Is this really the woman who has directed my dreams for the last half decade?

That's when it cuts me, a knife to the brain—Celia Favreau has gone off the deep end. She's crazy. Nuts. I shake my head, letting out a snort of self-pity at the pure waste of imagination I've heaped into my fantasies of her, and the choice I made to save her, the one that still haunts me a half decade later.

Self-pity, yes, but also a touch of relief, because doing this to a madwoman seems less wrong. We don't feel as much sympathy for people who don't see the world the way we do. We can't. And the ones who are certifiably insane—well, killing them is a kind of mercy. Arguably.

As I reach into my pocket to start up the recording again, I notice the wet handprint on the shoulder of my jacket. Treble has left his mark on me.

9

She's hanging up her phone when I come out of the bathroom, hand over my stomach, working my way toward her. Off to the left, Treble is taking out his wallet and examining his bill for inconsistencies. He doesn't look my way at all, and I wonder if, in my state, I imagined that whole conversation. It doesn't seem impossible, and for a moment it even seems likely. I settle into my chair and see concern in Celia's face. "You were in there a while. You're not sick, are you?"

I am, but I can manage another hour to see this through. I'll check myself into a hospital tomorrow, some place that specializes in the heart. "I'm good," I say.

"What's that on your shoulder?"

I brush at the fading spot, which, I realize, is the physical evidence that Treble really was with me in the bathroom. "Made the mistake of throwing a damp towel over my shoulder."

"You haven't changed."

I smile but say, "Was that Drew?"

"The phone?" She purses her lips and nods. "He's having trouble with Evan—who, I have to admit, has reached that demanding age. Chocolate is his current obsession."

"A reasonable obsession."

"No obsession is reasonable," she tells me. "When you're a parent you learn that pretty quickly."

I'm suddenly overcome by an urge I've never had in my life: the urge to reach over and slap Celia Favreau, née Harrison, across the face. I snap, "Enough with the lecturing, okay?"

Her smile remains unhurt. "Sure, darling." Then: "I've ordered chocolate mousse for you."

Our dessert menus, I realize, are missing. So be it. She wants to treat me like a child, then all right. The thought of chocolate turns my aching stomach, but I'll consume it simply to keep this madwoman happy. Because I'm back now. I'm ready to see this through and wrap up Frankler. "Tell me about internal investigations."

She thinks a moment, then sums it up with a single word. "Humiliating."

"How?"

"Well, it's their job to toy with your emotions. They played with my femininity. Lots of old-boy jokes. *Pretty girl like you in this business? How's it in the sack with that field agent, Henry?*"

"They said that?"

"Of course. They were supposed to knock me off my guard."

"Did it work?"

A shrug. "I told them you were so-so. Then I asked the big one if he wanted to give me a try."

"You *didn't*."

She's serious suddenly, and I have a sneaking suspicion she did precisely that, propositioned a man who had been sent to investigate her loyalty. I could imagine the old Celia doing that, just for fun. But she's shaking her head. "Of course not. I told them to piss off."

This, too, I can believe. It's the old Celia we're talking about, not the madwoman she's become. "What did they say about the phone logs?"

She stares into my eyes. "They didn't say anything about them."

"When you told them about the records, I mean."

Again, her head shakes. "I didn't tell them about the phone logs."

There. Finally, an admission. *For the record.* Overcoming my sickness, I give her a surprised look, the kind that innocent men like to use. "You didn't? Well, that's *odd.* Isn't it? I mean, they were trying to find out everything that happened, and you hid your own investigation from them. Why would you do that?"

She, too, senses that we've crossed a line. Her head tilts so she can get a better look at me. I wonder if she's kicking herself. "It didn't seem important, Henry."

"Not important? You suspected there was a leak. You tried to track it down. Then when Langley arrived to find out if there *had* been a leak, you hid your investigations. I'm sorry, Cee, but that kind of logic is beyond me."

I'm not sure what's going through her mind now. She

pushes her glass to the side, which makes me think she's going to reach across the table to touch me again. A part of me still wants that. A part of me even thinks that this—I mean, *we*—can still be saved. So very unlikely, but in the realm of distant possibility. Yet she keeps her hands on her side of the table and just stares, a sad smile turning the corners of her mouth. She blinks, and her eyes are moist. Is this the beginning of a breakdown, a sudden admission of . . . of what? Guilt? She says, "You know why."

"Do I?"

"Well, you looked over those records yourself. Didn't you?"

I'm trying to remember if I told her this or not. It doesn't matter. I nod.

"And what did you find, Henry?"

"Why don't you tell me?"

She inhales through her nostrils, then sighs. "You found a call at nine thirty-eight from Bill's phone. To Jordan."

"You saw it, too?" I ask, pressing.

"Of course I saw it."

"So you lied to me."

"We lie, Henry. That's what we do."

I feel a tingle of pleasure. Here we go. "You found this call, but you didn't tell anyone about it."

"I was going to, but then I changed my mind."

I wave that away. "Celia, I'm not going to be coy. This doesn't look good at all. Everyone in the embassy knows that two people used that office during the incident. Bill and you. The fact that you then covered up your findings does not play to your advantage. You need to give me a reason—a good, solid reason—for why you hid the evidence from the rest of us."

Her eyes are about to spill over with tears, but she's holding them back. She's also holding on to herself with her arms, defensive. She doesn't want to answer, so I continue.

"There are only two possibilities Interpol would consider here. A) You were protecting Bill, who you loved like a father. B) You were protecting yourself. So which is it, Cee? A or B?"

CELIA

1

First in Arabic, then in English, he says, "Everybody calm down!" But this is hard, because we've just watched him stand up and shoot the pretty stewardess—the one who served us drinks and cooed over Ginny and gave Evan a coloring book and crayons—through the chest. All of us watched as she skipped backwards in shock, then, realizing what had happened to her, she dutifully crumpled to the ground.

I'm not one of the screamers, but it doesn't matter. Six, maybe seven, women have taken over that duty for me. I suppose I'm lucky, having been trained for things like this. I know where my responsibility lies. When Evan says "What's that?" in his terrified voice and Ginny jerks in my lap and begins to cry, I turn back to them and pull their faces close to mine. "Listen. Okay? Are you listening?" They're nodding—unsure, desperate. "You will stay in your seats and be quiet. There is a bad man on the plane, and if you get out of your seats he will hurt you. Understand?"

They grab at me, pulling me closer, in the way they do that always makes me think they're trying to climb back into the womb. I squeeze them as if I can actually help them hide in there, where safety might lie.

"Everything will be all right. Okay? Mommy won't let anything happen to you. Okay?"

They're nodding with vehemence. The force of my voice has stopped Ginny's crying, but her eyes are streaming. Both of them are crying silently. My eyes have gone achingly dry.

That's when I see, up ahead, three more men climbing out of their seats, shouting for calm.

2

I wake, hands flailing, as my phone vibrates silently across the bedside table. On the other side, Drew is deep in retirement sleep, the one that lingers until late morning. For months after we moved, he continued to wake at six, as if there were still an office requiring his presence, but eventually the slow, hypnotic atmosphere of Carmel seeped into even his corporate brain, and now—eight thirty, I see—he's still out.

It's a +44 number, followed by 20—London. I carry the shivering phone into the living room, padding in bare feet across the pine floor, finally answering, "Yeah?"

"Cee?"

"Who is this?"

"Cee," the voice—old, faraway—repeats. "Celia, it's me. It's Bill."

"Bill?" I ask, briefly thinking that I'm still in dreamland, but I'm not. I never dream about Carmel. "*Bill.* Jesus, how are you?"

"Fine, Cee. Fine. You sound good."

"I sound confused."

"You haven't been confused a day in your life."

It's knee-jerk charm, for Bill learned to work with women from a young age. The only woman it never helped him with was his own wife, and this thought gives me a hopeful idea. "Is Sally all right? Nothing wrong with her?"

"She's fine. Excellent health."

Oh well. "Where are you?"

"London," he says. "We moved last year."

"But you hate London."

Silence, maybe embarrassed. "Well, it was important to Sally."

"Oh, Bill," I say involuntarily, though I know he doesn't want my pity.

"You have a minute?"

I'm in the kitchen now, pushing the phone between my ear and shoulder so I can fill up the coffeepot. "For you? Always."

"I've got . . ." He hesitates, breathing heavily. "Listen, I've been out of the game for over a year now, and maybe I'm just getting paranoid. But I thought I should call you."

The coffeepot is full. I shut off the faucet and pour the water into the coffeemaker, then lean against the counter. "Talk to me, Bill."

"It's Henry. Pelham," he adds, as if he has to.

"Go on." My voice has flattened. No one's said that name to me in years.

"He was here. In London. Putting me through the wringer."

"You? Why?"

"One-twenty-seven," he says, his own code for what the rest of us just call the Flughafen. I get off the counter and move to the dining room and sit down. "He tells me there's someone in Lyon asking for a full report, but I made some calls. He's lying. It's internal."

I wonder if I'm going to be sick. Not just Henry, but the Flughafen. And internal investigations. To calm myself, I look through the sliding doors to my backyard, where everything is in the eternal bloom of seasonless California. "Why did he lie?" I ask my flowers.

"To relax me, I suppose. But that didn't help. I . . . well, I broke. I'm no good at this anymore. He started laying down accusations."

"Oh, Bill."

"No, it's all right. I didn't handle it well. I'm out of practice. But I'm okay—that's not why I'm calling. You're the one I'm worried about."

"You don't have to worry about me," I tell him, because in a way I believe that. I've lived five years on the edge of the continent, and over those years I've shed one skin and grown into another. Marriage, children, and a new network of responsibilities in this lush village on the sea. I don't pretend the past no longer exists, but other than a visit from a man named Karl two weeks into our stay, and a phone call from him in June to tell me that an archenemy of world peace had been captured, the Agency has left me alone. Though I'm sure I still have enemies on the other side of the globe, none of them have been hurt deeply enough to seek revenge.

But this is Bill—he wouldn't say these things without a good reason. "What do you mean?"

"I think he's after you."

In the foreground the tulips are doing well, but farther back, between the jungle gym and the privacy fence, the hibiscus are in need of water. It's been a dry autumn. "How do you mean?"

"He played with me. He accused me of being in touch with the Chechen. Calling from the embassy. I panicked. I was playing to his script the whole time. It was just a way for him to push further and turn the conversation to you."

The magnolias are still in good shape, but I'm worried about pests. Around this time of year the moths appear in swarms, leaving eggs that will hatch in a week, sending out oak worms that will cover the trees and walls and doors as they devour everything in sight. I say, "How did he turn the conversation to me?"

"Did you ask for the phone logs? The embassy phone logs."

Instead of answering, I say, "Why?"

"Because he told me you did, Celia. He said there was a call from my phone to Jordan that first evening."

"I see."

"Well? Is this true?"

"Yes, Bill. It's true."

"And you covered it up?"

"Yes."

"But . . . why? You know I wasn't in league with those bastards! You *know* that. Right?"

I'm losing track of my garden. What needs to be tended to, and what doesn't? I lift my feet off the cold floor to the chair, raising my knees to my chin, one hand around my ankles, the other holding the phone. "At first, I didn't know. Not for sure. But soon afterward I knew."

"Then why didn't you tell me?"

"I should have," I admit.

"Yes," he says, then pauses. "Look, I didn't call to berate you. I'm calling to warn you. I thought I was under attack, all this about the phone call. Then he asked about you. Only after he left did I realize that he was just verifying what he already knew: that I didn't know about you checking the logs. He was narrowing down his suspects. Down to you."

It occurs to me then that we're on an open line. Though I haven't taken the possibility seriously before, I now wonder if someone is sitting in a landscaping truck up the street, listening to everything. I try to remember what we've said, what can be used as evidence, but the thump of my heart is distracting me. Then I hear something else—*"Mommy"*—it's Ginny's voice. I get up.

"Thanks, Bill," I say as I head back to the living room and toward her room. "I'll keep an eye out. Gotta run."

I hang up on him and push open the door to find Ginny, not quite two, sitting up in her bed, a white IKEA piece with raised sides to keep her from rolling out. Her hair is tangled across her damp face, and she's breathing in quiet sniffles, up from a bad dream.

3

I scramble eggs and gaze out at my garden while at the table Evan plays Angry Birds on the iPod and Ginny crunches toast slathered in peanut butter. Despite my fears, Ginny doesn't seem to be sick, and getting both of them dressed is a welcome distraction from Bill's call. Drew, ever old-school, brings a *Times* from the front yard and pecks me on the cheek as he throws away the paper's protective bag. "The liberal media machine is in full swing," he tells me.

"Is it?"

"Not that it's a surprise," he says as he settles at the table in front of his coffee. He shakes open the paper. "Old news is new news. Mitt made some innocent statements in Israel linking economic success and a nation's culture, and they're claiming—again—that he has contempt for Palestine."

I look up, frowning. "What?"

Drew grimaces at me, looking a little older and a little

stupider, but I know it's only a look. It means nothing. "It only took—what? Forty years?—for the Jews to build a great nation. That's not chance—that *is* culture. Mitt makes a statement of fact, and now he's a bigot."

I give him a smile, still not quite sure what he's talking about, but it doesn't matter. His phone will ring soon, and he'll head back to his office to work on the computer in defense of his dear Mitt.

"Mom?" says Evan, eyes not rising from the screen.

"Yeah?"

"Can I have Nutella?"

"No."

"Okay," he says.

Ginny, quite clearly, says, "One two three."

"Did you hear that?" says Drew, dropping the paper and smiling wildly. To Ginny, "Say it again!"

Ginny stuffs bread into her mouth, peanut butter a caramel-colored glaze across her cheeks.

"She heard it on *Sesame Street*," I tell him. "It's a song—One two three, count with me . . ."

"Still, though."

"Yes," I agree. "She's a genius."

From the bedroom Drew's cell phone rings. He gets up, saying, "And so it starts," then walks off.

I serve up the eggs, giving Evan the big-boy fork he's been demanding lately, and use the little-kid spoon to feed Ginny. But Evan doesn't want to break his game, so I take the iPod away from him and put it on the counter. "Breakfast first."

He groans.

Afterward, Evan takes his game into the living room and, after cleaning her off, I put Ginny in the playpen we keep by the sofa and tell Evan to keep an eye on her. Still fixated on exploding birds laying waste to green pigs, he grunts his acquiescence. I head back to the dining room and start to clean up.

It's while I'm at the sink, trying to get peanut butter off of Ginny's plate, that it comes back to me. Henry putting poor Bill into a state in order to direct an investigation in my direction. What's he up to? Is he trying to pin something on me? *That?* Unlikely. If he knows anything, he knows that I've been kinder to him than anyone. I've allowed him to live freely. And that, I realize now, may have been a mistake. Generosity sometimes is.

I take a breather and sit at the table, remembering our last night together. I remember standing at that pay phone and calling that number in Amman and hearing that voice speaking Russian and knowing—*knowing*—that it was Ilyas Shishani. Then returning to the embassy and sitting in Bill's office and thinking harder than I'd thought in a very long time. I thought about reasons. *Why* would Bill be in contact with a radical Islamist? Why would he give up our one asset on the plane? Money? Threat? Blackmail? Why would *any* of us call a member of Aslim Taslam to give up one of our own? It made no sense.

Did it connect somehow to Sally's pretend illness? Was she even in the hospital?

I called the Krankenhaus and asked for Sally Compton's room. After a moment, the nurse on duty said she would put me through. I hung up, then heard a knock on the door. It was Gene, his collar undone, bleary eyed. I waved him in. "Celia, there's something you need to look at."

I followed him back through the maze of cubicles to his desk and stood beside him as he shook his mouse, waking up his terminal. He was on the ORF Web site, an article with embedded video just under the title, in German, "Third Death at Airport."

"It's two minutes old," Gene told me as he clicked PLAY and raised the volume on his speakers. I leaned closer to get a better look.

It was low-light grainy, but clear enough to make out. A long shot of Flight 127 parked on the empty tarmac. In the darkness behind the plane lay an open, flat field and, farther, the lights of distant buildings. The whole airport had been shut down.

The camera was on a tripod, perfectly stable, and the image looked like a photograph. Then a hole appeared in the side of the plane—the forward entry door, opening. The cameraman, realizing he finally had something, zoomed straight into that hole, so we could see the shadowy form of a man standing in the opening. It was hard to make out his features, but he looked elderly, gray hair contaminating the blackness. White shirt, sleeves rolled up, and beige slacks. Mustache, dark skin. Then, without warning, the head blurred as if it had been knocked hard from behind—a distant *thump* sounded—and the man tumbled out of the doorway and dropped from the frame.

The frame jiggled as the cameraman tried to figure out what to do. It moved sharply down, so that we could see the body crumpled on the tarmac, then moved up again to the doorway. Another figure stood there, also dark-skinned, but much younger. We would later identify him as Ibrahim Zahir. Like the dead man, he wore a white shirt with rolled-up sleeves. He also held a pistol. A hissing sound filled Gene's speakers as the gain on the microphone was raised. The man shouted in English, "Take away your spy!" Then he pulled the airplane door shut.

"Mom! She's being bad!"

I break from my reverie and rush to the living room. Ginny's stacked her plastic building blocks against the corner of her playpen, forming an approximation of steps. She's standing on the top one and trying to get her leg over the edge of the gate. At that same moment, Drew wanders in and says, "Look at our little genius!"

Evan shifts on the sofa so that his back is toward us. I worry he's getting jealous of the attention his little sister is showered with. Drew goes to pick up Ginny, and I continue to the bedroom to change. As I slip into jeans that once upon a time were loose on me, I open my laptop. As I'm buttoning my blouse, the machine dings an incoming e-mail. When I see Henry's name, I have to sit down. He's going to be in my neck of the woods.

4

Two days later, I'm sitting at a picnic table on the terrace outside the Carmel Academy of Performing Arts while Evan is inside taking ballet lessons. He's the only boy in his class, but it took only a couple of lessons for him to get over this fact—he's the center of attention. Ginny is safely with Consuela at My Museum, getting active and social, which means I have forty-five minutes to make up my mind. From my purse I take out the white, embossed card I was handed two weeks after we arrived here. Just the name in small caps—KARL STEIN—and a phone number.

I haven't answered Henry's e-mail yet. What I know and what I suspect about his interests are muddy, and it's taken me two full days to decide what's to be done. I called Bill, and his answer was definitive: "Do not meet him under any circumstances. Don't give him an opening."

But Bill speaks from fear. His desire is to run from all fights. He's retired, after all, and all he wants is peace during his final years. I can understand this, because unlike Drew I want the same thing. The last thing I want is to be drawn into Henry's double-dealing. There's a significant difference between Bill and me, though. I have children, and once you have children your life begins all over again. You start to take care of your health and welfare with a new imperative—the imperative to be around to protect them from the world. It's no longer about living well now, but about living well for as long as humanly possible. Therefore, a quick fix is no solution. Problems must be dealt with head-on. Threats must be neutralized.

I've already made up my mind, yet I still hesitate. It's something in the air, and in the leafy beauty all around me. It's in the quiet calm that has come to define my life, even when the kids are acting up. There's a silence here, between the words, that I've grown to depend on, and if I make the call it'll be shattered.

There's no choice, though. Not really. If I withdraw, Henry will follow me because by now he's desperate. He's terrified in the way that only the truly self-absorbed are, and I won't be able to shake him so easily. He will come here. He won't just shatter the silence; he'll try to shatter everything that I have.

So I take my phone and type out Karl Stein's number. As it rings, I wonder if the number's still in service. Maybe he's switched phones, and I'll end up talking to some teenager who's never heard of Karl Stein and is only worried about getting a call from some girl he's crushing on. Maybe this will be harder than I expect.

I needn't worry—he answers on the fourth ring.

"Karl Stein," he says.

"Karl, hi. This is Celia Favreau. We last talked in June, and—"

"Celia," he says with a rising pitch to his voice. "Cee to her friends. You still living in paradise? Carmel?"

"Yes. I am." A mother and daughter are lumbering up the stairs, the girl's tutu stained with grape juice. I turn away and lower my voice. "Do you remember the conversation we had some years ago? About Bill Compton."

"Of course, of course," he says, all joviality. "I also remember you told me to go fuck myself."

"Sorry."

"Happens more often than you might think. Don't worry about it."

"Listen," I say, realizing I can't say it all on this phone. "I need to talk with you. But not on an open line."

"You want me to fly out there?"

"Maybe. Well, not if it's not necessary."

"I always like an excuse to get out of the office," he says, all old-boy in-jokiness, then settles down. "But if you just want to talk securely, I can text you an address in Pacific Grove. You go there and ask to use the phone. Sound like a plan?"

"Sounds fine," I say. "I'm not sure when—"

"Ginny and Evan," he says, and I imagine he pulled up my file as we spoke. "Kids do put a strain on our time."

"You're not kidding."

"No worries. Just call as soon as you get a chance. I'll have my phone on me 24/7."

"Thank you, Karl."

Not until that afternoon, after a black woman leads me up the stairs of a Pacific Grove condo to a simple little room with an encrypted satellite phone, and I'm finally able to use all my words to tell Karl Stein exactly what my problem is, does it occur to me that Karl probably has kids himself. Unlike Henry, he knows that the world is a lot bigger than his own needs.

5

I wake, terrified and swinging, but instead of Suleiman Wahed I'm hitting Drew. He's saying, "Celia! *Celia!*" and trying in vain to catch my wrists. The orange haze clears, and my fists slow down, finally allowing him to catch them. He holds my hands tight and watches my face until my breaths gradually come under control. My back and face are drenched in sweat. "Hey," he says. "You with me?"

I nod, and he lets go.

He props his head on a hand, elbow in his pillow, watching as I sit up. "The plane?"

I nod again and get to my feet, then keep walking until I'm at their doors. I check on them—first Ginny, because she's smaller, then Evan. They are exactly where I left them last night, untouched. In the bathroom I strip out of my wet nightie, splash water on myself, dry off with a spare towel, and head back. The clock radio tells me it's five in the morning. Drew's eyes are closed, but when I climb into bed he opens them. "Want to tell me about it?"

"I want to go back to sleep."

"Have you talked to Leon about it?"

"Of course," I say, not wanting to get into it. "But I don't need a shrink to tell me why I dream about that plane."

"Maybe you need one to help you stop dreaming about that plane."

He's trying be helpful, I know. Constructive, the way he once ran his arm of the General Motors Corporation, seeking out problems and banging them back into shape. But I say, "Don't start."

"Start what? I just think you shouldn't have to suffer."

How to explain it to him? Could I tell him that my hope is that after this evening I won't be cursed by this dream anymore? No, because he'll ask why. He'll want to know how dinner with my old lover will translate into peaceful nights. Then, because I can't tell him more, I'll have to deal with his jealousy, for a man of his age can't help but see a threat in every younger man who comes along. So I just turn my back to him and close my eyes. "Don't worry about me," I say.

I wait for the sound of him settling his head back on the pillow, but it doesn't come. Just silence. He's staring at the back of my head, waiting. Sometimes this man drives me crazy. So I turn to find him watching me with glazed eyes, as if he's about to weep. But Drew Favreau doesn't weep—it's not in his DNA. This is as close as he gets.

"What?" I say.

"There's something going on, and it has to do with Henry. I'm right, aren't I?"

"Nothing's going on. Go back to sleep."

I'm not the liar I once was, so it's no surprise that he stares at me a while longer, unbelieving. I lean close and kiss his lips and say, "Really, Drew. I just have bad dreams. Henry is nothing. Not to me. And that's something you can take to the bank."

He nods at that, gives me a sad smile, and puts his head down. I give him another kiss, on the cheek, then lie down, my back again toward him.

Later, when Evan is at ballet and Ginny at home with Consuela, I'm at Safeway, walking down the aisle of freezers stocked with frozen pizzas and ice cream. I think about Drew. By breakfast he was over his insecurity, but I'm not sure I am. He's a perceptive man, and this last week he's sensed my growing anxiety, my sudden bursts of bitchiness, and my too-long silences. Hopefully by tomorrow I'll be recovered. More likely, after tonight I'll have days, or weeks, of regret that will translate into more mood swings, but eventually things should settle down. Life will return to normal. We'll be able to move on. He'll help his candidates, and I'll raise our children, and only the future will matter to us.

"I love me some Häagen-Dazs," says a voice behind me, and I turn to find a young man with long sideburns, the way men wore them in the late sixties and young men are starting to do again. They call themselves hipsters. This hipster is named Freddy, and he's opening a glass door, scanning the varieties on display.

"Where's Karl?"

Freddy doesn't turn to look at me. "With these cameras? He'd like to meet you over by the UPS Store." He takes out a pint of chocolate chocolate chip.

"Is everything all right?"

"Perfectly, Mrs. Favreau. Everything is good to go."

I use the self-checkout to buy a bag of tortilla chips, then leave it on the passenger seat of the SUV and walk the rest of the way through the Crossroads shopping center, an open plaza of upscale and boutique shops that services the whole of Carmel-by-the-Sea. A pedestrian walkway takes me past clothing stores, a bookshop, and a café. At the crosswalk, I see Karl sitting on a bench in front of the UPS Store, a paper coffee cup in his hand. Beyond him, beyond the low stores, rises the mountain range that forms Carmel Valley.

There are no cameras out here, but plenty of cars drive by. I wonder about his idea of security.

Random gusts of wind buffet me as I cross the street to sit next to him. He's smiling. A genial fifty-something, gray-haired, in an open-collared shirt and blue slacks. California business casual. "This place is gorgeous," he tells me.

"The UPS Store?"

"Ha ha," he says. "Your town. I always liked it."

"Freddy tells me everything's all right."

"Well, yes," he says, but without much conviction.

"What's wrong?"

He uses an index finger to wipe something out of his eye. "Well, nothing, really. We got Rendez-vous, just like you suggested. Private party, charged to a Big Sur company. But I don't like that we can't put up a sign to keep everyone else out."

"He would know," I tell him, yet again. "Trust me, though—tonight you'll get two, maybe three, customers. The place is completely out of fashion. You do have a chef, right?"

"Flown in from D.C. She's excellent. Jonas will be running the bar. But there's a hitch. You know Jenny Dale?"

I shake my head.

"Well, she's their regular waitress, and the owners are insisting we use her. She needs the work, apparently."

"Then give her some money."

"We tried that," he says. "She got suspicious."

I squint into a fresh gust of wind. "Really?"

"She wanted to know why we didn't want her there. Why we'd be willing to pay her without using her services. She's . . . well, she's *weird*. I mean, who gets upset about free money?"

"Is it going to be a problem?"

He shakes his head, then shrugs. "Depends. If she figures out what's going on, then it's going to be a big problem."

"Who else knows?"

"You, me, and Freddy. Jonas and the chef think it's a surveillance op. We'll let them out the back before the job's finished."

I think about this. "If the chef doesn't know . . ."

"Freddy's taking care of it."

I nod. That about covers it. But he's still looking at me, as if for guidance. That's when it occurs to me that I'm the one running this, not him. I'm the one who called him. In that Pacific Grove town house I was the one who told him what I thought was going to be necessary, and that's exactly what we're doing.

Karl clears his throat and says, "We're right about this, aren't we?"

It takes a moment to figure out what he means. "Yes," I say. "He's the one."

"Because I've been wrong before. Like with Bill Compton—I had that one ass backwards, and you were right to tell me to fuck myself."

"This time," I tell him, "there are no mistakes. We are in the right."

He sips his coffee and thinks about that. It seems funny that I have to be the one to reassure him. It's supposed to be the other way around.

6

First in Arabic, then in English, he says, "Children to the front!" We're in row 22, but he's seven rows up at 15, shouting at a black woman who's clutching her five-year-old boy in a bear hug, shaking her head no, as if the command has made her mute. But the boy's not scared. He's kissing his mother's forehead and whispering something into her ear, something that relaxes her shoulders. He slips out of her loosened grip, takes the hand of Ibrahim Zahir, and walks with him to first class.

"The front!" says a voice behind my ear. I turn to find Suleiman Wahed, face pinched and splotchy, a gun in one hand, looking into my soul.

I rise halfway out of my seat to block his view of Evan and Ginny. "No. Not them."

Do I really believe that this will be enough? I do, actually, and so I'm taken off guard when he says, "You give them to me now, or I'll kill them in front of you."

Would he? A face like that, he might. So I stand completely still and think it through. I measure distances—between me and the back of the seat, between his gun hand and my hand, between my children and his gun. I wonder how long it will take Ibrahim Zahir to get back to us, and how long the other two hijackers, Omar Ali and Nadif Guleed, would need to run out of the cockpit. I give Suleiman Wahed a hard look and say, "You take them out, then."

I'm exasperating him, and I can feel the anxious attention from all the other passengers. What kind of lunatic would provoke men with guns? *Give them up,* they're thinking. *Hand them over, you crazy bitch.*

Roughly, with strength that makes me doubt what I'm able to do, he pulls me out of the way, into the aisle, and leans forward to grab my children. Ginny screams. It's a high, department-store-alarm scream that digs into the eardrum, and it's my cue.

I throw myself on Suleiman Wahed's sloped back, arms on either side of his head, fingers clawed, and grab both cheeks, ripping. Nails tear into soft skin, and he lets out a howl as he stumbles back. I'm riding him in the aisle. He tries to shake me off, but now my thighs are around his waist. I grab his chin with one hand and slip the other to the back of his skull and pull with all my strength, just as the pirate taught me. A delicious crack sounds inside his neck, and he drops, me falling with him.

It all happens so quickly that Ibrahim Zahir, walking the black boy to the front, is just now turning around. I'm fumbling with the gun in Wahed's death grip, finally getting it loose. Then I raise it. We've drawn at the same time, Zahir and me. Our shots explode in the enclosed space, so that the ringing in my ears cuts out most of the screams around me. But Zahir is down now, convulsing on the floor, as the little boy stares at him, stunned.

I stay low, moving quickly toward the boy, waving him out of the way as the cockpit door opens and one of them steps out—Omar Ali, I think. He carries only a knife, which glints in his right hand. One shot.

Bang!

Down.

The door jerks as I reach it, Nadif Guleed trying desperately to close it even though Ali's body is in the way. I take a breath and rip open the door and shoot him once in the face, step into the cockpit, and shoot him again.

I'm gasping now. I haven't moved this quickly in years. I lean against the cockpit wall, staring at the mess at my feet. This is what death looks like—messy, wet. It's what you have to look at in order to appreciate the opposite. It's what you need to do if you love your children.

Then I notice how silent it is.

Not silence, really, just no voices. A hissing sound: the ventilation. The lights in the cockpit are on, and though I see the crowns of the two pilots in their chairs, their blue caps above the headrests, I don't see their faces because they haven't bothered to look at me.

There it is, like every time, the crushing weight of knowledge.

I straighten and balance on my own two feet, so tired. I step over Omar Ali's corpse, back into the cabin. Up in the front are six children, ranging in age from two to nine, pale faces in stark contrast to the blood running out of their noses and, in one case, covering a girl's chin. My focus stretches out, reaches back, and the dead fill the whole length of the plane. I run down the aisle, counting rows, and when I reach 22 I nearly trip over Evan's sneaker sticking out in the aisle. His limp foot is inside it. He's on the floor, having slipped out of his seat during his death tremors. Ginny is rolled up in the seat above him, in a puddle of something dark.

HENRY

AND

CELIA

1

She's not answering, so I lean closer. "*Who* were you protecting, Cee? Bill? Just tell me. If we don't answer this question now, then it's going to come back. Maybe not now, but in five years, ten years. And next time it won't be from a man who loves you."

When she blinks, a tear comes out, and she wipes it with the finger that wears her wedding band, an unostentatious strip of white gold. She sniffs. "You know, Henry. This is why I left Vienna. It's why I married Drew so quickly and got the hell out of there. The fucking Flughafen. At first, I thought I could get over it. I thought life could return to normal. And it did—but that was the problem. Normal, in Vienna, meant the constant pressure of secrets. It meant living in a maze. It meant not even trusting the people you loved. And guilt, so much guilt. A hundred and twenty people dead." She snaps her fingers. "Like *that*. Doesn't it tear you up?"

"It tears all of us up."

She shakes her head. "I don't think it tears you up, Henry. No, I don't think it bothers you all that much. What did I tell you about love? There's only one kind of love that's real, and this . . ." She points at me, and then herself. "This isn't it. It never was."

She's confusing me again, and I look away in order to gather my thoughts. Treble is counting out dollars and placing them in a tray, moving with the exacting motions of the miser. In the corner, beside the empty bar, the replacement waiter with the sideburns is watching him closely. Once Treble's left, she and I will be alone. A part of me fears this. The other part, my defiant half, says to Celia, "I think you're giving yourself too much credit. I didn't come here to sweep you off your feet. You hid crucial evidence about a leak in the embassy. I'd like to know why."

Her eyes are dry now, touched with red veins, and she shakes her head. "Henry, we both know Bill didn't do anything wrong."

"And what about you?"

"Me?"

"If you weren't protecting him, then you were protecting yourself. Is that how you want it to read in my report?"

"It's galling," she says, her voice dropping an octave and taking on an edge that I haven't heard yet tonight. "I mean, I'm trying to play this off until the end. I'm really trying. But you're obstinate to a degree that I can't quite comprehend. All this diversion. Do you really think it makes any difference in the end?"

I stare at her. There's no anger there, not really, just frustration, and this is what worries me. I'm cornering her, shoving her around with the growing accusation, and she's not reacting as she should. She should either break down like Bill or rise up with a muddled defense. Because I have her. I really have her. She found a crucial piece of evidence and went out of her way to keep it under wraps. She's carried this secret with her, hoping against hope that it would never be uncovered. But Gene Wilcox gave me the direction, and a simple look into the logs told me what I needed to know: She saw the phone call. Bill admitted that she never brought it to him—that recording is on my computer in Vienna. So we come down to the culprit herself. It might not be courtroom evidence, but we don't bring things to court these days. It's enough.

Does she know? Does she know who that businessman is who's getting up from his table and walking past her to the front door, muttering "Thanks" to the waiter without even a glance in my direction? If she did, she wouldn't be so composed now. No one would. The door closes. Treble's gone, and we're alone.

No, it doesn't really make any difference, because I've made my decision, and very soon Celia won't be around to defend herself anymore. What I'd like, though, is a final answer from her before the job is finished. The final justification that I'll be able to use if Vick or someone at Langley connects the dots to figure out what I've done. We can't let traitors off the hook, and we can't prosecute them. I'm only following Agency logic to its inevitable conclusion.

"No," I tell her. "It doesn't make any difference in the end. But I'd like to hear it from you. I'd like to hear you tell me that you made the call to Ilyas Shishani and told him about Ahmed. That you killed our only chance of getting those people out alive."

"Did I?"

She's cool now, tears gone. Hardening right before my eyes.

She says, "I'm not sure what you think you can do here tonight. I've been able to figure out some of it, but not all. You obsess over one small thing—me neglecting to inform everyone that someone used Bill's phone to call Shishani. You fixate on this, and then you go corner Bill. You get him to admit he doesn't know about it, which means that if I didn't tell him, I didn't tell *anybody*. Right? Very good. But where next? Do you think that the only conclusion that can be reached is that I was in cahoots with Shishani?" She shakes her head. "Have you really been that cloistered?"

"You tell me, then," I say, standing up to her despite a resurgence of pain in my stomach. "Tell me what other conclusions there are."

She smiles again. She straightens. "You know what I thought when I found that phone number? I thought the obvious—Bill had been selling us out. I didn't understand why, or how he'd ended up roped into this mess, but he was guilty. Then Ahmed was killed. I was beside myself. So I came straight home—to your home. To you. You remember?"

I blink at her. My vision's a little blurry, but I don't want to start wiping my eyes. I don't want her to think I'm getting teary. "Yeah," I say. "I do remember."

Because I do. I remember every act of sex we engaged in. I've lived off of those memories.

She's nodding slowly. "That, Henry, was when I knew."

2

He's pushing into me, hauling up my left leg, gripping my ankle in his sweaty hand. Straining. The veins of his strong neck are standing out in the darkness, and down here below it feels like he's splitting me open. This is all my doing, for when I arrived at his apartment I said nothing and went straight for his body. And it's nearly working; it's almost enough to push away Bill's sad face and the gut-wrenching betrayal I feel. All I want to do is escape into sex, so that I can disappear and not have to face questions of moral outrage. I want it all to be simple. A boy and a girl fucking in an unmade bed with the Viennese night hanging outside.

Then it's over. He's gasping beside me, saying something about what kind of apartment he thinks we can afford, how close to the Danube, and what a crazy good idea it is. I say, "Sure. Yeah," but I'm still stuck in indecision. I want to tell him about Bill. I want Henry to sit across from me, still pink-skinned from all his exertion, and make it simple for me. Either: *A traitor is a traitor, Cee. You've got to bring it to Vick.* Or: *This is Bill we're talking about. Let's take it to him first.* I want him to take responsibility for deciding what to do, because in Moscow he became familiar with betrayal and trickery, while in Dublin I lunched with émigrés and danced to electronic music and learned how to stomach heavy ales without getting sick.

When he gets up, kisses me hard on the mouth, and tells me he's going to shower, I wonder why he doesn't see my indecision. Can't he read it in my face, or is it too dark in here? How long does it take for a man to learn the ciphers of your moods? A year? Ten? Never? I suppose it's something I'll be finding out.

As the hiss of water runs in the bathroom, I pull on my clothes and stumble into the kitchen, where only this morning I made coffee and thought about leaving Henry. Now I'm staying, and I just want a little coffee so I can think through everything rationally. I fill up the machine with water and grounds, then turn it on. That's when I hear the *d-ding! d-ding!* of a phone ringing. It's not mine, nor is it the melody of Henry's Nokia. Frowning, I step out of the kitchenette into the living room and pause, listening. *D-ding!* Then nothing. Yet it's enough to send me over to the coat rack, where my overcoat and Henry's hang limply. I pat Henry's coat—in the breast pocket is a hard lump. I pull it out just as the screen illumination is turning off, a flash of phone number disappearing. No, it's not Henry's regular phone. It's a Siemens. Gray and too big to be comfortable. It's the second phone that all field agents keep—prepaid in cash, anonymous. But I haven't seen this one before, so maybe it's a simple burner, to be thrown away once the minutes have been used up. Before putting it back, I press the menu button, and the screen lights up. Along the bottom of the screen it asks me to unlock the phone in order to use it, and right above the request, in the middle of the screen, it says MISSED CALL and displays a long phone number that begins +9626.

It doesn't hit me then, not entirely, and this delay is a sign of either my exhaustion or my feelings for Henry. I wonder offhand where the call is from, but the smell of brewing coffee has reached me, and I'm more interested in that. I put the phone back in his pocket and turn toward the kitchenette before stopping in the middle of the living room. +962—Jordan. 6—Amman.

I take out the phone again and look at the number. And I know, because when I discovered Bill's treachery I kept looking at the number, trying to find ways for the digits to rearrange themselves to prove his innocence. They never did. Now I'm reading that number on Henry's spare phone.

"Where are you?" I hear, but it's back in the bedroom. With adrenaline pumping in my head I replace the phone and rush back to the kitchenette. The pot is half full. Trying to control my voice, I say, "Making coffee."

"Good idea," he says. "I'm going to have to hit a club downtown, see if I can't find some Moroccan I've been hearing about."

By now he's walking down the hallway toward me, clad in a waist-high towel, smiling, hair glistening.

"What's wrong?" he asks as he reaches me, two strong

hands touching my shoulders, then sliding down to my elbows. His breath smells minty.

Everything is wrong, but for him I choose a single tragedy. "Ahmed was killed. I found out just before I came here."

His smile wavers, sliding away, and then he purses his lips as if he's trying to keep something in. Is he? "Shit," he says, then repeats himself. *"Shit."* He gives my elbows a final squeeze and turns away, heading back to the bedroom, not letting me see his face. Only now, after that phone number, do I wonder about this. He says, "I'd better get moving, then."

I want to follow him. I want to corner him in the bedroom and tell him more. Tell him, *They told us to take away our spy. They knew. How did they know, Henry?* But I don't do that, because for the first time in our relationship I'm scared of Henry Pelham. So I stay in the kitchenette and pour two mugs of coffee and drink one as I wait for him to come out of the bedroom. When he finally does, he's dressed, and I hand him his cup. Distractedly, he thanks me. What's he thinking? Is he thinking of a Moroccan he needs to track down? Or is he thinking of Ilyas Shishani, his controller? Is he thinking—and this just occurs to me—that the one thing he needs to do is to make sure no one captures Shishani, so that he isn't implicated?

"What are you going to do?" he asks.

"Go home, take a nap, then get back to the office."

"You can do that here, you know."

I nod, feeling like the only thing to do is to agree with him. "If that's okay with you."

He smiles as he comes over and gives me a kiss that

now tastes of coffee. "We might as well get started on co-habitation."

I smile back and watch as he opens the drawer beside the oven and takes out his spare keys. Ceremoniously, he places them on the counter. I tilt my head regally to show that I recognize what this moment represents.

When he puts on his coat, I come over and, like a dutiful wife, smooth his collar. I'm really very good at this. He grins. "Off to work, honey!"

I give him a quick kiss on the cheek. "Go save the world, darling."

Then, five minutes after he's left, I run to the bathroom and vomit.

3

The story finally out, she just stares at me, and I'm not sure what to do. This is what has kept her strong this whole dinner. It's why I've been unable to make her break down like Bill.

Did I know? No. Or maybe I suspected it. Maybe I had the feeling, after her sudden departure from my life that night, that it wasn't just a fear of commitment pushing her away. And maybe this is why I've been so fixated on bringing the investigation to her doorstep and getting whatever I can out of her first. I lean back, not quite trusting myself to speak. I shift my legs, noticing the lump in my pocket.

Shit.

The phone. It recorded her whole story. I reach in and find the power button and press it long enough to be sure it's off. I'll have to edit it later, before I turn it over to Vick. *If* I turn it over to Vick, because I'm not sure there's enough on there to incriminate her. Because now, I realize, I have no choice. I will tell Treble to go ahead and take care of it, and by the time he's finished I'll be on a plane heading home, or rushing to some all-night clinic to deal with my fucking upset stomach. If Vick traces it to me, he will just have to believe whatever version of this night I choose to tell him.

Celia says, "You're not going to deny it, are you?"

I sniff, look around the restaurant. We're the only customers, and even the staff has disappeared into the kitchen. We're completely alone.

She says, "You were the one who knew Shishani from before. You were the only one with a connection to him. And you knew this left you vulnerable, so you went into Bill's office and called that number, just in case. Plant disinformation on the off-chance someone started investigating."

"Where's this phone?" I ask, working off of hope now.

"What?"

"Nice story," I say. "Nice way to turn it around. You see that number on my phone. But where is this phone? Do you *have* it?"

"Really?"

"What?"

She sighs. "That's really your defense?"

I shrug, mouth shut.

"What I'd like to know," she says, "is why. I'd like to hear this now, before I go home." She cocks her head. "You were a decent guy, Henry. You didn't stab people in the back. And when the job forced you to betray people, it hurt you. Was this about Moscow? Were you getting the Agency back for what happened there?"

Despite myself, I shake my head no.

"Then what was it? It certainly didn't make you rich. And I don't really think you went for all of Aslim Taslam's nonsense."

In the far corner, I see our waiter looking out at us. I say, "Where's that chocolate mousse?"

"Forget the fucking chocolate," she says, vitriolic now. "You're not getting dessert. Now tell me."

"I'm not going to tell you anything, Celia."

She looks past me and, feeling suspicious, I look over my shoulder. Nothing, just the front door, with blackness in its glass. Then I see two figures emerge from the dark—a middle-aged couple in matching blue windbreakers. Tourists. The man reaches for the handle, but it doesn't budge. It's locked. The woman taps him on the shoulder and points at a small sign in the window that, from our side, says,

Come in we're

OPEN

They're reading the reverse.

"What time is it?" I say as I take out my cell phone, the regular one. It's only nine thirty. I've been here two and a half hours. I pocket the phone and find Celia's eyes on me again. The other phone, the one that is fatal in so many ways, is no longer recording a thing. So why not? Evidence doesn't matter anymore. Maybe facts will suffice. Maybe we're finally in that quiet space where all the masks fall away and we're left with just our skin. So I say, "I did it for you, Celia."

She flinches, as if I've raised a threatening hand. *"What?"*

"You can sit there and judge me. But I did it for you. And then you walked out on me. After everything that happened on that plane, how do you think I felt?"

She opens her mouth, closes it, then says, "I don't understand what you're saying, Henry."

"This isn't a riddle, Cee. I did it for you."

But it is a riddle, in a way. Both her hands are on the table, pressing down. "Please spell it out for me."

Though it hurts in my midsection, I lean closer. "I did it to save your life. What I did killed many more, and in a way it killed me, too. But I saved you. I saved you because I thought we were going to be together. Then you walked."

4

I rush through the apartment and find everything of mine. Underwear, toothbrush, sanitary pads, the works. I stuff it all into my purse, swallow coffee, and rush out. Remembering, I go back in and scoop up the keys from the kitchen counter and leave again, locking up this time. I find my car on wet Florianigasse, and only after I get inside do I think to be wary. I look around, wondering if he knows what I know, then wondering what that might mean. I wonder if all this recent affection, this invitation to move in with him and to start envisioning a future for us—is all this just a way of taking me off the scent?

But no—his old Mercedes is gone. And, no—he doesn't know. How could he? For all he knows I'm waiting in the apartment, pining for him.

I start to drive back home before changing my mind and returning to the embassy. It's four thirty in the morning, and I half expect the place to be empty. But of course it's not. Bill is still gone, but Vick is in his office, making calls to America. Ernst is catching a nap in his office, feet propped up on the corner of his desk. I even find Owen sitting in the break room when I get more coffee. He says, "I didn't expect to see you."

"I'm like a dog," I tell him. "Always come back."

He tries on a smile; it doesn't fit. Mine doesn't, either.

"Anything?" I ask.

He shrugs. In front of him on the table are a sticky roll and a cup of milk. He eats like a child. "Merkel flew her prisoners here, so now they've all been collected. Some prison outside of town. They're not telling us which prison, which we're not happy about."

"They're probably not happy we waited to tell them about Ahmed."

He shrugs.

"Are they going to give in?"

Owen takes a bite of the roll. "Ernst doesn't think so. He says that it's just a ruse to buy time."

"Then what's the plan?"

"Well, the attack is off. They're scared of Ahmed's last message, before he was killed."

"Do we believe it was him?"

Another shrug. "I don't. But the Austrians don't take my word as gospel. The question is," he says quietly, "how did they get him?"

Despite myself, I settle into the chair opposite him. "What's the answer?"

He raises his brows. "You? Me? Ernst? Bill? Or maybe he just did something stupid."

Here it is, my first chance to say it, but I don't. Instead,

I give a pleasant smile and climb to my feet and wander back to my desk, just outside Bill's office. I settle down heavily. I yawn into the back of my hand and wonder why I'm not marching into Vick's office and giving up my lover. My ex-lover. Because that's what he is now.

Yet I'm saying nothing. Why? Is love really so stupid? Bill's love certainly is, locking him up tight with a monster. And mine? Maybe it is. Maybe—and this is a new thought, a sort of revelation—this is the problem. Maybe love is the wrong way to live. Maybe anything that infects good sense is to be shunned. It's a possibility I'll examine closer, when there's time.

Now, though, I have to let my good sense take over, so I swallow a last sip of coffee and get up, coming out of my self-absorption in time to notice that the office, even running on a skeleton crew, is noisy. Ernst is crossing from one side of the floor to the other—from his office toward Vick's—and Leslie is leaning over Gene's desk, shouting, "Ask them! Don't go on hearsay! Ask them if it's true!" Owen is walking out of the break room, a paper napkin to his mouth, his eyes on the floor as he listens to one of his young code breakers talk quietly into his ear. I go to Leslie, the closest, and break into her tirade. "What's going on?"

Her eyes flash at me, and I read hatred there, as if by interrupting her I've broken international law. I've never met this Leslie before. She says, "Go ask Daddy," then turns back to Gene and says, "Follow up with Heinrich! Now!" Gene types frantically.

I follow Ernst to Vick's office, and through the blinds I see our chief of station with his chin on a fist, elbow on his desk, watching Ernst march around the room, talking and waving his hands, so that he looks more Italian than Austrian. In the open cabinet, the television is set to ORF, as it has been all day. I knock on the door and walk right in. Ernst says, "I told you. I told you all—" before stopping to glare at me. I ignore him.

"What is it?"

Vick raises his head and leans back, stretching. "Close the door, Cee."

I don't know if he wants me inside or outside, so I just close it behind myself and stand waiting. Ernst is glaring. Vick says, "The Austrians think they're dead."

"Who?"

"Everyone. The passengers, the hijackers. The crew. Everyone."

What I imagine at this moment is an explosion, a great fireball of destruction, but on the muted television a local government official is signing some kind of legislation. "How do they know?"

"They don't know, not for sure. But about five minutes ago—"

"Ten," Ernst corrects.

"Ten, right. Well, they started up the engine. The plane didn't go anywhere, didn't light up, but the Austrians started receiving signals. A message came through. *Aslim Taslam does not negotiate.* The engine is still running. They've got hi-res cameras focused on the cockpit, and they recorded the pilots dying. Both of them, sitting right in their seats."

"Shot?" I ask.

Vick shakes his head sadly, and Ernst, impatient, breaks in. "No one touched them. They suffocated."

"Respiratory failure," Vick says, as if that makes it any clearer.

I look from Vick to Ernst and back again. "They turned on the plane," I say as it crystallizes in my head, "to start up the ventilation system."

Vick nods slowly. "That's what we think. It's what the Austrians think. But we can't go in if we don't know."

"Sarin," Ernst says. "It's sarin. They need to order doses of atropine and pralidoxime. *Now.*"

"Maybe," Vick says.

But this time Ernst is right. I can feel it.

5

She says, "A hundred and twenty people killed. What? For *me*?" She shakes her head. "You *are* talking in riddles, Henry."

Of course I am, because after years of silence it's not easy to say these things aloud. But maybe she deserves the real story, the truth behind the truth, the kind of thing that, once upon a time, was her bread and butter. Maybe a final wish is in order. Maybe—and I know how desperate this is, how adolescent—if she knows, she will understand. For a moment, I hold on to that thought. I let my childishness take over and embark on a brief journey into an alternate future. It begins with me telling her, in detail, exactly how I saved her. Her guilt, as she finally comprehends what she's done to me, is accompanied by tears. She gets up and crouches beside my chair, holds on to my aching stomach, squeezing, her tears marking my shirt. She pets me, then climbs up, whispering *Thank you,* and begins to kiss me with grateful fervor. Then she takes my hand and says, *Let's go.*

This fantasy is the most enjoyable moment of the day, but I can see from her face that even in close proximity there is no psychic connection. She never felt my late-night molestations, and she feels nothing now. She is on a different plane. I say, "I talk in riddles because that's what I deal with every day."

Not even a hint of a smile. No acknowledgment of my wit.

I reach a hand across the table, but there are no slender fingers for me to grab. She stares into my eyes, as if my hand doesn't exist. I say, "You have no idea what I went through. After you left. You have no idea—"

"Your *feelings* were hurt?" she snaps, and my hand draws back. "You had a broken *heart*? You want me to cry for you? Is that what this dinner is about?"

"No, Cee. Listen. I—"

"Shut *up*!" she shouts, holding up a hand, flat, palm facing me. "Enough, okay?"

Over in the corner, I see the waiter leaning back against the kitchen door, arms crossed over his chest, watching my humiliation. I've still got some pride, so I raise my chin at him. "You like watching, asshole?"

Impassive, he retreats into the kitchen, but not before a smile slips onto his face. Then it occurs to me that he hasn't brought us the bill. Or maybe he brought it when I was in the can, and Celia took care of it.

She's not even looking at me now. She's leaned back, arms across her stomach, and is staring past me at the front door again. If we were a comic strip, she would have a black scribble of smoke above her head. Still looking past me, she speaks quietly, as if only partly to me. "When they were all killed, I didn't know what to do. I thought . . . well, I don't know exactly what I thought. Maybe you were innocent. Maybe it wasn't Ilyas Shishani on the other end of that phone number. It was some other Russian speaker. I can't say I believed this, but I wanted to believe it. Stranger things have happened. So I buried it. I buried the call from Bill's phone in order to protect you. After all, they were dead, weren't they? Putting you in front of a tribunal wasn't going to bring them back to life. Was it?"

I watch her looking past me and say, "We don't do tribunals these days."

"I know," she says. Her eyes are wet again when she focuses on me. "But then you chose that one piece of evidence—the phone call—and scared poor Bill half to death. You thought that by making a call from his line you would frame him . . . or me. But I'm betting you didn't know that by pushing the issue you would hang yourself. Did you?"

"Nobody's hanging me," I tell her.

She smiles at that—actually smiles—and says, "If that's what you want to believe."

Though I made up my mind a while ago, it's now truly apparent that I can't go back on the decision. Celia will not survive this night. She can't. She's put it all together, and though she put it together years ago and said nothing, I can't depend on her silence now. Therefore, the decision is not really my decision. It's an evolutionary choice. Either I abide by the need for self-preservation or I die. There's no decision at all.

So it doesn't matter. Enlighten the doomed. "Do you really want to know?"

She blinks at me, waiting.

6

It is December 7, 2006—two months after the murder of Anna Politkovskaya in her Moscow elevator, two weeks after the death of Aleksandr Litvinenko in London, his bald, hospitalized head a fixture of the press during his month-long battle with polonium-210. It's not about blame—these deaths are certainly not my fault—but about association. How the reminders of Moscow can draw me back into the grinding duplicity that, in the end, is how I define that chapter of my life.

I wake with Celia looking down at me. She's smiling, and with the anxiety that overwhelms me these days, I react to that beautiful face by covering my head with a pillow. She leaves to get coffee, and I scold myself. I've been doing this for weeks, each newspaper and Internet site reminding me of Moscow, and as a result I've been pushing her away. Occasionally, she asks what the problem is, but I don't want to speak about Moscow. I don't want to make it any more real than it already is.

So I say nothing, and when she returns with steaming cups we talk about our plans for the day. I pretend to care, because I know that in my right mind I *do* care, particularly about her. That's when I notice a blinking light on my phone. A waiting message says

Schloss Schonbrunn—GLORIETTE—10.00

There's no doubting what it is—a request for a meet at the Schönbrunn Palace, at the axis point of the gardens. There's a café there that I've visited a couple of times, but never for work. Who am I meeting? I don't know the number.

So I cut the morning with Celia short and drive westward to reach the sprawling palace grounds, which in the blustery winter are empty. I fight the wind heading across the park. The Gloriette section is closed for the season, but the gate is unlocked, and when I reach the imperial arches of the Gloriette itself the door to the café is also unlocked. I open it, looking into the dark interior, where chairs and tables have been stacked against a far wall. It's dead. Then I hear it: the click of heels against tile. A man in a heavy, quilted coat emerges from behind the dark counter, limping and smiling, saying, "Henry!"

It takes a moment to process his face. He's aged in the past four years, his dark features ashen and gray. He's grown fitter as well and, in the way of thin people, more intense. He looks like a weary but improved version of the man I knew in Moscow. He's smiling, approaching me rapidly, a hand out. I accept it, and we shake. Unexpectedly, he embraces me and kisses my cheeks. "Ilyas?" I say. "What the hell are you doing here?"

I'm scared—I know he's no longer the gentle baker I once met with, but he's doing a good job impersonating that once-innocent man.

"Come," he says, his voice full of warmth, pulling me deeper inside. He grabs two chairs from the wall and sets them on either side of a table. "I'm sorry—they've cut off the electricity, so there's nothing warm to drink. But I remembered," he says, taking from his deep coat pockets two plastic bottles of Coca-Cola. "You still drink it?"

"Not often enough," I say, accepting one and sitting across from him.

How do I feel? It's complicated. There's fear, yes, but more. I'm unnerved, for out of the past one of those Moscow faces has emerged, one of the few I was actually fond of. But Ilyas was part of those Russian conversations that ruined me. Ilyas was one of those insidious compromises that forced me to finally flee Russia.

"What are you doing here?" I repeat.

His smile doesn't leave. "You look so good, Henry. Imperial cities become you."

"And you're in excellent shape."

"Thank you," he says, shrugging as he drinks his Coke. I drink my own; it burns. He says, "Looks are deceiving. I've got a limp, you saw. A present from Vladimir Putin."

"Putin?"

He smiles again, toothily, and takes out a pack of Marlboro Reds. He offers one; I decline. He lights his. "I am only here briefly," he says. "To see you."

"I'm honored, Ilyas." Though I'm not. The shock is wearing off, and I'm left with what has become of Ilyas Shishani: I'm sitting with a wanted terrorist.

He raises the smoldering cigarette next to his ear. "Do you remember Moscow, Henry? We had what could best be called a tense relationship."

"I don't remember it that way. We had conversations."

"Yes. But do you remember how it started out? When I wasn't sure I wanted to share what I knew with an American? Remember what you said?"

Of course I remember, but I say nothing.

"You told me that all it took was a phone call, and the Russians would be on me in a heartbeat. You used that word—'heartbeat.' So I cooperated. Yes, we had some laughs, and yes, you did donate some money to my life, but our relationship was defined by that first conversation. 'Heartbeat'—that word never left my head," he says, tapping his temple with his cigarette hand. "You see my point?"

I blink at him, not sure I can do much more than blink. "Sure. I get it."

"You remember," he goes on, "how you told me about trust? Yes, you even defined it for me, as if it were a new concept. I have to tell you, it wasn't. I was very familiar with it. But later, I realized you were right—it did need to be defined. You understand?"

I shake my head. "No, Ilyas. I don't understand."

"Well, maybe you do need help remembering. Because not long after those terrible fifty-seven hours at the Dubrovka Theater there was a knock on my door. No," he says, shaking his head. "Not a knock. A sudden *boom*!"

He claps his hands together, sprinkling ash across the table. "Boots! Seven men dressed scalp-to-toe in black, with automatic rifles. Spetsnaz—very tough men, you understand. The Russians brought me in, and for two months I did not see the sun. Two months, I am not kidding. I was questioned. I was tortured. My leg," he says, tapping one of them, "was broken and reset badly. I was accused of being a terrorist. Me! A terrorist! Can you imagine? Timid little Ilyas, the Chechen immigrant who bakes bread for a living and gives away his friends' names to the Americans . . . a *terrorist*? Perhaps you told them I was a terrorist?"

I shake my head. "I would never tell them that."

"No," he says, waving his cigarette, "I didn't think you did. This would not be in your interest. Apparently, though, you *did* tell them everything about our relationship. Because, you know, my interrogators told *me* all about our relationship. Told me things that not even surveillance would be able to discover. This, I have come to realize, is the American definition of trust."

There it is. In the intelligence world, when you betray people you endeavor to do so only to organizations that know how to keep a secret, because it's more important to keep an image of innocence than the reality of innocence. The FSB had not bothered to protect me. So, staring into his weary eyes, two bottles of Coke between us, I tell him the truth. It's the only defense I have. I was under orders, I explain. It was a politically tricky time. "I protested. Afterward, I wrote a letter of complaint to Langley."

He raises his hands. "Oh! A letter! And *afterward*! That

does make me feel so much better, Henry. I didn't realize you were such a prince."

He's right—I know this. Were I in his shoes, I wouldn't be so kind. I wouldn't sit down to have a chat with the person who had betrayed me. I might invite him to the Gloriette in order to give my act some regal splendor, but I would not talk. I would come out from behind the counter with a baseball bat and crush my betrayer's legs, arms, and skull. This conversation, I think, shows that Ilyas is a better man than I am.

I don't know how much time passes—twenty minutes? An hour? I tell him details, painting the entire picture of the schizophrenia of foreign policy in Moscow, the anxiety in the embassy, my frustration. Admirably, Ilyas allows me time to say it all. Only afterward will it occur to me that he predicted all of this; my speech is right on schedule. When the excuses finally cease, he says, "Look at me, Henry."

I do so, but it's hard.

"You and I," he says, speaking slowly so that I can understand everything, "are forming a new relationship, and this is the conversation that will define it. Are you listening?"

"Do I have a choice?"

He smiles. "Of course you have a choice. You always have a choice. You can walk out of here right now and wait to find out what you didn't want to listen to."

"Okay, I get it. Tell me."

"Good." He leans back and lights his third cigarette. "This is what we will do. You will give me a phone number that I can use to call you. One of your untraceable phones. Using that number, I will call sometimes to ask for information, and you will give it to me. You will see the number I'm calling from, but that number will not lead you to me. Very simple, no?"

I look at his cigarette, the glowing ember, and say, "It sounds simple, but I'm guessing it's not. Let's say I refuse."

He raises the index finger of his free hand. "Yes! Now we get to it. This part is actually very simple, too. If I call you and you refuse to answer my questions, then Celia Harrison, that beautiful woman you share your bed with, will die." He sits up straight, almost boyishly excited. "In a heartbeat."

7

I listen to this, the slow story, so full of details, and I can see him growing weaker. It doesn't matter that what I'm doing is justified—it still breaks my heart. I want to get up and go, but it's not time yet. I want to leave all of this behind and never look at it again, but I know now that it doesn't work that way. I'll carry this night for the rest of my life. I'll flash on it while I'm putting Ginny to bed, and when I'm watching Evan's ballet recitals. My job will be to make sure it doesn't suffocate me, because that's what kids do—they force you to keep going.

I'm surprised. Of course I'm surprised. While I don't want to believe it—while I want this to be another of his lies—I think about those crowded Viennese streets. How many shadows trailed me that day? Was Ilyas Shishani among them, or only the men who reported to him? No, he wasn't watching me himself—he was too busy organizing the murder of a hundred and twenty people, and making calls to my lover.

But this isn't what gets at Henry. He's not haunted by the deal he made with Shishani—he's haunted by what followed. Not the murders, but the end of our relationship. It's a monstrous level of selfishness, and I want to tell him this, but the words don't quite make it out. He's being broken down enough tonight.

"What do you think?" he asks.

I think that I hate you. I say, "You were in a difficult situation."

"That's all?"

"That's all."

Behind him, through the window, I see Karl walking up the sidewalk and stopping at the front door. He uses keys to unlock it, and the noise of the tumblers distracts Henry. He turns back. "Who's that?"

Though he doesn't really need an answer, I tell him. "It's Karl. With a *K*."

He frowns, thinking. Given his condition, it comes to him very quickly. "What's he doing here?"

"Watching over me."

Henry looks back, but Karl doesn't come in. He's only there to unlock and guard the door, so that I can leave. Freddy emerges from the kitchen and goes from window to window, closing the blinds. Henry sees this, too, and he sighs. "You set me up."

"You tried to do it first."

He looks bad. His skin is a pattern of crimson and alabaster. I take my purse from the back of the chair and hold it in my lap, looking at him.

Henry says, "*Shit.*"

While it is not part of the script, I tell him, because

given our history and what's to follow, it feels like the right thing to do. These days, I try to follow my conscience more often than my calculations. I'm still working at it. "Henry, listen to me."

He's glaring at me.

"Your veal was poisoned. You don't have much longer."

This time he's slower on the uptake. His features contract. He shakes his head, and I can tell from his expression that the movement aches. It's so hard to watch someone die.

I say, "You know how it is. They don't want a trial."

He looks back at Freddy, who's closed the last of the blinds. But Freddy, too, doesn't want to watch any of this. He takes a pack of cigarettes out of his pocket and goes out the front door to join Karl.

"You're killing me?" he asks, his voice weak and innocent. "You're . . ." He doesn't finish the sentence.

"I'm sorry," I tell him, because I am. Then I stand up. I can't watch this anymore. "Thank you, though."

He looks up, eyes beginning to leak their tears, veins running through the white orbs. "What?"

"For not letting Ilyas Shishani kill me," I say. "It was the wrong decision, but I do appreciate it."

Unexpectedly, the corner of his lip rises in a half smile. "Don't be too thankful," he says. There's bitterness in his voice, but less than I would expect.

"Good-bye, Henry."

He doesn't reply. I walk out of the restaurant on rubber legs, trying to keep myself straight, sure that he's watching, though when I reach the door and look, his back is to me. He's staring at the far wall, just sitting there.

Karl opens the door for me, and I step out into the cool night. "Well?" he asks as he closes the door.

"He knows."

Freddy shakes his head, smoke drifting out of his mouth, and Karl says, "You *told* him?"

I nod.

He peers through the glass door. Henry is still sitting. "Well, I suppose it doesn't matter. Five minutes, maybe ten, then we'll go in and clean up."

I nod.

"You can go home, if you'd like."

I'd like. "We're done?"

He raises his hands, palms out. "Done. You need a ride?"

"I need to walk."

"Fair enough."

"What about the waitress?"

Karl rocks his head. "That was a mistake. She figured out what was going on. Inevitable, I guess, with the way we kept trying to turn people away, and the fact that no big party arrived. But the problem was that she saw Freddy dosing the veal."

"My bad," says Freddy.

"Yes," Karl says disapprovingly. "Anyway, I don't think she understood right away, but on the way to your table she put it together." He shrugs. "Admirable, really. She was thinking on her feet. Not many people like that."

"So what happened to her?"

"She's fine," he says. "Don't worry. We're just trying to figure out what to do with her."

"Don't hurt her."

"Hurt her?" He grins, waving the idea away. "I'm of a mind to offer her a job!"

We look up at the sound of footsteps. It's a young man in a long coat, his hair glistening—it looks like it needs a good wash. I assume he's going to keep going, but he stops beside Freddy and says, "Thank you, Celia. You've done us a great service."

"Who the hell are you?"

He doesn't look like he wants to answer, but Karl speaks for him. "Larry's one of us."

I don't care anymore. I don't care who anyone is, or whether or not they think I've done a good job. I just want to go home.

I look inside again. He's just sitting there, elbows on the table, as if he's a deep thinker—which he isn't, not really. Or maybe he's already dead.

8

She walks right out of my line of sight, but I don't turn to watch her leave. I'm trying to remember that word, the one she used to describe the kind of person she was. Yes: jettisoner.

I have been jettisoned.

I place my arms on the table and press my fingers together. When, I wonder, did I lose control? The beginning, I suppose, when I first laid eyes on her, getting up from that bar over there. *Are you leering?* she asked me, and she had me figured out. But the beginning wasn't tonight—it was six years ago, when love strong-armed me into a pact with Ilyas. Not only love—guilt, too—but still. Or even earlier, sitting down with Ilyas in the back room of his bakery in the Arbat District, offering him my Marlboros, and saying with wild confidence, *We've got this thing in America we call trust.*

I have to go to the bathroom, but I'm too tired to stand. So I let it go, a warm blush down the inside of my thigh.

As if it matters, I take the Siemens out of my pocket and place it on the table in front of me. A gray dead thing.

I'm just thinking, dreaming really, of everything. Of the one-eyed instructor at the Farm, crouching in the mud of the obstacle course, shouting pirate wisdom. Of an ankle in my hand, the knotty protrusions pressing into the meat of my thumb. Of sweat. Watching the footage in Vick's office of the first Austrian cameraman entering Flight 127, the bodies frozen in chairs, scratching at the windows, lying in the corridor. Of Celia's barren little apartment, so empty of history. That final call from Ilyas after the sarin had killed everyone—*You've helped the cause of God, Henry. That is no small thing. You will be rewarded in Heaven.*

But I don't believe in Heaven.

Then it doesn't matter either way, does it?

It matters, I realize as a sharp ache cuts into the back of my head, blinding me for a second. It matters because doors are closing everywhere. The door to Bill's office, to my Viennese apartment, that plane on the tarmac, this restaurant. When they all close, there will be nothing left. Water turning to steam, swept away by the clean sea breeze.

I wish I could go down to the beach. I hate this restaurant. I don't want to die here.

What was the right decision? Let her die back then? How could I have done that? How could I have known what they were preparing to do? How could I have predicted what would come next?

Then I'm thinking of her children, because those are what really took her from me. Those little monsters turned what she had with me into a mere shadow of what she has with them. What did she say? *Beside it, romantic love is cute. Passion is just a little game.*

Oh, Christ. I can't feel my legs anymore.

From somewhere, I hear *d-ding! d-ding!* It takes a moment, because my eyes are closed now, and I haven't received a call on that phone in years. I open my eyes and see the little screen alight. I can't read what it says, and I wonder if it's her, calling to tell me it was all a joke. But how would she know this number? I pick it up.

"Hello?"

"Piccolo."

"Uh, yes."

He waits, and I know I sound different. He's waiting for me to verify who I am. I'm not sure who I am—I'm trying to listen for my heartbeat. I'm failing.

I say, "Yes, Treble."

"Listen," he says, breathing hard, "I've got her. Right here in front of me. She's just walking down the street. Very slow. I think she's crying."

"Oh," I say.

"If you want it done, now's the time. I don't know when I'll get another opportunity like this."

"I see."

"It's up to you, Piccolo. There'll be nothing left. I can do this clean."

When I cough, my throat burns. I say, "Natch."

"What?"

I blink. Someone's turning down the lights in the restaurant, or maybe it's just me.

TURN THE PAGE FOR AN AUTHOR INTERVIEW ON

ALL THE OLD KNIVES

WITH OLEN STEINHAUER

Q: Sorry for the trite question, but where did you get the idea for *All the Old Knives*, which is so different than anything you've done before?

OLEN: As I mention in the preface, it was a simple matter of admiration that led to imitation. I was living in Carmel, CA, when on PBS I came across *The Song of Lunch*, a dramatization of a Christopher Reid poem, which itself tells of a London editor past his prime who's going to lunch with his ex-lover, who is now glamorously married to a famous writer. It takes place mostly around a restaurant table, and yet it is, for the length of its hour, utterly mesmerizing. It doesn't hurt that Alan Rickman and Emma Thompson are at the table, but the narrative's emotional leaps and twists are what carry you forward. I wondered if I could limit a spy novel to a dinner table. And after a half year of letting the idea percolate in my subconscious, it finally came out in a flood.

Q: Was it difficult for you to write on a such a smaller canvas than you usually do?

OLEN: To be honest, it was a real pleasure to strip it down this way. Some readers complain that they need a scorecard to keep track of the characters in my books, and on rare occasions I do, too! But also the geography is limited: a restaurant in California and a handful of locations in Vienna. That said, I was in semi-uncharted territory and had to find ways to raise the tension without adding other characters, or cutting quickly to Saudi Arabia. The story is rather simple, and it was just a matter of organizing it the best way possible.

Q: Was developing such fully realized characters harder to do at this length, both in terms of number of words but also in terms of a time line, meaning with so few events to work with?

OLEN: Like I say above, it became an issue of organization more than anything. I quickly realized I had two parallel stories and two parallel perspectives, and knowing when to present one or the other, and when to cut away, proved the most difficult. But in terms of character I still had plenty of space in which to flesh them out—this book is half the length of my usual books, but with about a quarter of the characters. In the end it wasn't very hard at all.

Q: Do you yourself have more sympathy for Henry or Celia?

OLEN: Depends on my mood—which is, I hope, how most readers feel.

Q: Was the ending of *All the Old Knives* hard to write? Were you tempted to take the story further? Did you have a scenario that you decided not to include, or did you always plan to end the story here?

OLEN: I knew what would happen in the penultimate scene, but I didn't know how far I would push the very end. There was a lot more that I could have told—not just about Celia, but about the mysterious recordings that crop up here and there—but it came down to feeling: I simply felt that the story had run its course, and to push it further would kill the rhythm. Unsurprisingly, when I wrote the screenplay for it, I did add a little more, because in film there's a tendency to feel cheated if you're not given the full denouement.

Q: You recently have finished writing a film script based on *All the Old Knives*. What was the process like of translating this novel to film? How different was the process from writing a novel? Was it hard to transfer this story, which has plenty of internal activity, from page to screen?

OLEN: Well, like the composition of the novel itself, it was easier than expected. In fact, it only took four months to get a decent draft together. Despite so much of the movement of the novel being internal, it turned out that most of the necessary details were spoken or could be signified easily through action. Of course, the roles will demand a pair of excellent actors to bring those extra nuances to life! What I think is most difficult is if there is too much action in a novel, and you have to decide what to throw away. In this case, I was able to keep most of the book intact and just focus on reorganizing its presentation for the screen.

Q: Henry seems to have a little bit in common with Milo Weaver, the hero of your previous trilogy, in that he is one person Milo could have become if he hadn't chosen to leave that life. How much do you go into your stories intending to write about the morality of the espionage world?

OLEN: As far as I'm concerned, examining the psychology and morality of the job is the only reason to write espionage fiction. It's why I was able to spend three books—and, eventually, there will be more—looking at Milo Weaver without ever feeling like I was repeating myself. The flashy stuff—the guns and gadgets and tradecraft—are only there to serve the inner stories being told.

Q: Does the fact that Celia is a parent make her a different kind of "spy" than Henry? Or is it that she's female? Both?

OLEN: Beyond espionage, parenthood is *All the Old Knives'* other subject. As a parent myself, I've been frankly shocked by the level of devotion a child earns without doing anything at all. And what Celia does in the story has nothing to do with her gender, or even espionage: She is simply a parent who will do anything to protect her brood. Which, I think, makes her a typical parent.

Q: Do you find that what interests you in writing espionage changes from book to book? Or are there timeless themes or conflicts that you come to again and again, in the guise of different scenarios?

OLEN: I think the latter. While each book may be framed by different subject matter, the basic themes and conflicts repeat, particularly when you're dealing in a particular genre. Questions of trust, loyalty, betrayal, and, really, existential meaning are things that pop up continually in my work. It probably says less about the genre, though, than the person writing. Writers can be stubborn, slow-witted creatures. We ask ourselves the questions that obsess us, then ask again in the next book, and then the next. Which only goes to show that novels do not present answers; they present possibilities.

READ ON FOR AN EXCERPT FROM
OLEN STEINHAUER'S *NEW YORK TIMES*
BESTSELLING NOVEL *THE LAST TOURIST*

PART ONE

EXPENDABLE TURTLE

7 8 9 0

TUESDAY, JANUARY 15, TO THURSDAY, JANUARY 17, 2019

1

It's easy to forget, now that so many facts have been laid bare, but we once lived in a state of holy ignorance. We didn't believe this to be the case. No, we studied the world and examined facts and argued over their interpretation. We took newspapers with a grain of salt, because to depend on strangers for knowledge was foolishness. Verification was our go-to word. We even debated whether or not the facts themselves could be trusted, and this sort of meta-analysis made us feel like we were truly critical, that we were looking at the world unencumbered by Pollyanna notions. We were wrong. Sometime over the past fifty years the center of the world had moved, and we hadn't noticed.

You would imagine that I'm talking about regular people, citizens going about their days focused on bread and love and children. I could be, but for fourteen years I had worked as an analyst for America's premier foreign intelligence agency, and even in the halls of Langley, armed to the teeth with secret information and specialized enlightenment, we wallowed in the same kind of ignorance. We made policy recommendations and sent employees out into the world, sometimes to die, based on a basic misunderstanding of how the world functioned.

For half a century, we were distracted. We let the wrong people grow stronger, so that by the time we were able to look directly at them and see them for what they were, it was too late to draw up search warrants and set court dates and frog-march them in orange vests to Leavenworth. That would have been a better, cleaner solution.

I joined CIA from graduate school in 2005, seduced by a pale poli-sci professor who had spent a mysterious part of his youth in Prague. Though my stated interest, when asked, was international relations, that was only an excuse to get at the thing that truly excited my younger self: secret knowledge. Fieldwork was naturally attractive, but I'd quickly discounted myself. My social skills have always been lackluster, my physical courage less a known fact than a hypothetical, and confrontations have never gone well for me. In short, I was temperamentally unfit to be a spy, but I knew how to strategize, and I knew how to analyze. Despite my inability to charm them, I understood people because I had always observed them from the outside, as if through a microscope.

It helped that I looked different. In Boston, among the pink-cheeked children of America's aristocracy, or the striving descendants of the African labor that had built the country, I was never quite one with any of them. My skin set me apart from the former, my lack of enslaved pedigree from the latter. When I told them my people were Sahrawi, they blinked ignorantly, and I knew I could fill that void with whatever I liked. That we were Saharan royalty, that we ran caravans loaded with gold, that we kept our own slaves. I didn't, but I easily could have. And when my older brother later died in the African hinterlands, I could have made that part of my mythology, too, but I didn't have it in me to do that.

What my professor understood, which I hadn't, was that this outsider status was precisely what would endear me to the Agency. He said, "You were born here, but your parents weren't. How does that feel, Abdul?"

I told him that it made me feel mildly schizophrenic. My soul was in this country, while my heart was tied to a place I didn't know.

"And you speak Arabic."

"Hassānīya Arabic, yes, and I've studied modern standard."

"Do you dream it?"

I smiled, shrugged, nodded.

"Photographic memory, I'm told."

"No. Just a good one. Like, I don't have to take notes at your lectures."

"I've noticed," he said. Then: "Sunni, yes?"

Four years earlier rogue members of the Sunni faith had declared war on America in an explosive fashion, so it was inevitable that I hesitated. "I was raised that way," I told him.

"How does that make you feel?" he asked pointedly.

I was unsure what he was getting at. "It makes me feel that the world is more complicated than people believe."

He might have pressed further but chose not to. Instead, he moved to the core of his pitch: "And you want to understand how the world really works."

"Doesn't everyone?"

He rocked his head, chewing the inside of his lip. "No, Abdul. Not everyone. Most people don't. But I can connect you with people who *do* understand."

Which is to say that he fooled me, just as he was fooling himself, because fourteen years later neither of us knew how the world really worked. We only looked at it through a more sophisticated lens and believed that our lens was the highest resolution that could be achieved short of divinity. Belief usually isn't enough.

In the outside world, what some would call the real world, I'd fallen in love with another first-generationer, Laura Pozzolli, a beautiful linguist with a biting wit and an instinctive sense for right and wrong that I could never match. By January 2019, we had been married seven years. Our son, Rashid, was six.

There is nothing like a family to help you discover the limits of your abilities. At the office I swam like a shark from one project to the next, my analytical skills put eagerly to the test against country after country, yet at home I was a turtle, graceful in one moment, struggling on muddy banks the next. The tension between home and work did not get better with time, and when the phone periodically rang in the middle of dinner and I had to drive off to examine time-sensitive cables or captured documents from terrorist safe houses, the look on Laura's face told me more than her occasional outbursts ever would: This was not what she'd signed up for. She'd been raised by a Communist father who had always endeavored to take on half of the child-rearing himself, and when her parents met me they warned her that, no matter how good my intentions, I would inevitably fall back on the ways of my culture, leaving her with the babies and housekeeping. We'd laughed about that, though I never told Laura that after meeting her my mother criticized the girth of her hips, then pointedly asked in Hassānīya how many grandchildren she could expect.

I'd like to say that I worked overtime to alleviate my in-laws' worries, but when I look back there's little sign I really tried. When Paul, my section chief, called, I never said no, and when Laura pointed this out I asked her who she thought was going to pay the mortgage. Quite rightly, she accused me of becoming my father.

It was on such a night that the phone rang, and Laura glared at me from across the table as I answered it. Rashid was twirling spaghetti on his fork, unaware of the tension. By the time I hung up, Laura was covering my plate with plastic wrap on the counter. I told her I didn't know what time I'd get back, but that wasn't news. Security prevented me learning anything until I'd arrived at headquarters.

2

On the cold drive to Langley, I listened to NPR. For the past three weeks, the president had refused to fund the government, demanding money for his southern border wall, leading to a shutdown of basic government services. Then the news turned to the Russian-tainted 2016 presidential election; Nexus founder Gilbert Powell had testified before Congress on his company's extensive safeguards against foreign attack. Unlike his contemporaries from Facebook and Google, Powell soothed his audience with a mix of charm and perfectly remembered statistics. I couldn't help but wonder, as I drove, if tonight's cable or fresh intelligence might touch on this or another of our current national obsessions.

The interconnected offices of Africa section are in the original building, looking every one of their seventy years. As I passed through security there was no visible sign of the government shutdown. Agency work went on as usual.

Paul was in his office, the air bone dry from the overworked radiators, with two women who chose not to stand when he brought me inside. Though they were vague about their positions and only shared their given names—Sally and Mel—it was clear that they were creatures of the seventh floor, because Paul always deferred to them, something I'd only seen in the presence of the director himself.

"We have an issue in Western Sahara," Paul told me.

Sally passed over a thick yet heavily redacted file. Inside, I found a graying white man staring back at me. Oddly familiar—where had I seen him? Late forties, though photos on later pages (surveillance shots on mildly familiar European streets, one in Manhattan) suggested he was older. The flesh around his eyes was dark, and his long nose, in one shot, looked as if it had been broken. On the third page I found his birthdate—June 21, 1970. His name was Milo Weaver.

Most of the things I learned in that office didn't come from the blacked-out file but from Sally and Mel. They explained that Weaver had once been one of ours, though no one wanted to tell me which department he'd come from, and in 2008 he had left to work with the United Nations. Again, no one wanted to tell me whether or not the split was amicable, and the page that might have told me this was a mess of thick black lines. The only entirely unredacted page was in the back, a list of twenty questions that began:

1. Please list your locations between October 4, 2018, and today.

October 4 . . . yes, now I remembered—Milo Weaver's face had shown up on an Interpol Red Notice in October. The Red Notice, as far as I knew, was still live.

"These questions are for him?" I asked.

Mel, a tight-lipped Latina in a beige pantsuit, tilted her head and nodded. "Weaver's been on the periphery for years. We catch sight of him in the background at UN functions. Periodically shows up at their New York Headquarters. Supposedly part of UNESCO, but we know better."

"I don't. What does that mean?"

She ignored my question and pushed on. "Then in May of last year, he was in New York meeting with the Bureau."

"With Assistant Director Rachel Proulx, out in the open," Sally picked up, smiling grimly.

"The *Bureau,*" Paul said contemptuously.

The women grinned; everyone enjoyed teasing the FBI.

"Rachel Proulx," I said, remembering newspaper headlines and cable news talking heads. "Wasn't she connected to the Massive Brigade case?"

"Yes," Mel said.

"Why was she meeting with UNESCO?" I asked.

"She doesn't talk to us," Mel said bitterly. "But Weaver—you'll see in the file. Long history with the Massive Brigade. In fact, he saved Martin Bishop's life in Europe ten years ago, and continued to help him, all the way to 2017. A lot of people are no longer with us because Weaver aided and abetted that terrorist."

It didn't make any sense. Why would the UN help a radical group that we'd put on the terrorist list? Or was this Milo Weaver acting independently? Either way, it was a damning connection. Martin Bishop's Massive Brigade had terrified the nation for a long time until the FBI took out its leadership. But then, unexpectedly, the remnants of the Brigade rose up, as one. Their second reign of terror last year had spread with bombs, shootings, bank robberies, and demonstrations that crippled whole cities, all led by a stern-looking middle-aged acolyte named Ingrid Parker. Her face had been plastered across every screen and front page for months; she became the representative of chaos. The last big act they committed had been in June, when a truck bomb exploded outside Houston's Toyota Center during a basketball tournament, killing three. And then, for the last half year, silence. Not a single sighting or online screed.

"I thought the Massive Brigade was disbanded," I said, because this was what everyone assumed.

Mel looked over at Sally, who raised her eyebrow. "Well," Sally said, "we've got word from the Germans that Ingrid Parker was seen in Berlin. Coordinating with European radicals."

"Which would explain their silence," Mel pointed out. "We might not know what they're up to, but you can bet it's big."

I tapped the file. "And you think Milo Weaver can tell us what it is."

"Bingo," Mel said.

Sally leaned closer. "He dropped off the grid in October. Then, yesterday—three whole months later—we find out he's in Laayoune, Western Sahara."

"Why there?"

"Why do *you* think, Abdul?"

Laayoune, which the Spanish called El Aaiún, is the capital of the disputed desert expanse just south of Morocco called Western Sahara. It's where my people come from. Yet despite my knowledge of its industries and history and culture, I was no expert on the city itself. The closest I'd ever come to it was a disastrous week in Rabat with my brother, Haroun, in 2000, when I was still a teenager. We'd been looking to connect with our heritage. A mugging and a visit to a questionable brothel was as close as I'd ever gotten, though Haroun returned to explore further and pushed on, making it all the way to Laayoune. He, however, was no longer available, and it looked like I was the most qualified person in the building.

"Milo Weaver is there because it's an excellent place to hide."

This seemed to satisfy them, in the same way that we're all satisfied when experts give us unequivocal opinions. We forget that everyone has an agenda, even if it's as mundane as keeping their jobs.

"And the position on the ground there?" asked Sally. "I'm not familiar."

I gave them a quick history lesson. In 1975, after controlling the area for almost a century, Spain handed it over to Morocco and Mauritania. By the next year, the Polisario Front had proclaimed an independent Sahrawi republic and was at war with both countries, supported with arms from Algeria. Mauritania pulled out in 1979, and in 1991 the UN negotiated a cease-fire with the promise that Morocco would hold a referendum on independence the next year. "Twenty-eight years later," I explained, "that referendum still hasn't been held, and the UN's peacekeepers—MINURSO—are still there. But violence hasn't broken out. Yet."

"Didn't you write something for outside publication about this?" asked Sally.

She knew about my one academic credit, a short piece on Sahrawi identity under French and Spanish domination, published in *Foreign Affairs* a couple of years ago. "Tangentially. The important thing is that Western Sahara remains disputed territory, and people are impatient."

"So there's no one for us to piss off," Paul said.

"Everyone's already pissed off," I said, and that earned smiles from Sally and Mel, whoever they were.

"Your, ah, brother," Mel said, for the first time sounding unsure. "He passed away in that region, yes?"

"South of there. Mauritania. 2009."

"What was his job again?"

Again? It was a peculiar word to slip in, a subtle way of rewriting history. "Consultant. For foreign investors. He worked most of the continent. I'm told he was good at his job."

"Right," Mel said, nodding, and it struck me that even though they were coming to me for answers, they still weren't sure they trusted me. As if Haroun's loyalties might say something about my own. But he'd been gone ten years now, and few people can maintain loyalty for so long.

"Who told you?" Sally asked.

"What?"

"That your brother was good at his job."

"I cleared out his desk at Global Partners. His coworkers were devastated."

Sally seemed to accept that, and Mel chewed the inside of her cheek. Paul cleared his throat and said, "Rest assured, Abdul. We'd feel the same."

By the time I returned home, midnight had come and gone, and Rashid was asleep. Laura was watching television. Over the last few years political news had become a spectator sport, and like any spectator sport it brought us together even when we weren't otherwise talking. I sat with her a moment as a so-called expert in security discussed progressive groups that were using some of the protest techniques invented by the now-defunct Massive Brigade, and there again was the face of Ingrid Parker—hard and unforgiving. They flashed through shots of Massive Brigade graffiti, its initials stylized as M3, as Parker, in her half-year silence, had gained the stature of a folk hero. More than anything, I wanted to tell Laura what I'd heard, that the Massive Brigade might be ready for a revival, but I only told her that I had to leave for a couple of days. "I'll be back by the weekend."

"Where?"

"Africa."

"It's a big continent," she said, but knew I couldn't be more specific. She turned back to the television. "Your shirts are in the dryer."

3

By the next day, I was dragging my carry-on through the busy Terminal 2 of Mohammed V International Airport, outside Casablanca, looking for *pastilla,* a chicken-and-*werqa*-dough pie that, after seventeen hours of travel, was the only thing I craved. Greasy bag and pile of paper napkins in hand, I sat near a large family of six children and two wives, watching how the patriarch, a heavy, grizzled man, sat with his knees open, his gut hanging over his groin, and a phone pressed hard into his cheek, talking quietly while chewing a toothpick. One of his wives sat on a bag "nexting" (as Rashid called it) with N3XU5, or Nexus, the social media app that boasted absolute privacy—no GPS tracking, encrypted text and video, and no message retention in the cloud—and had become ubiquitous outside North America, to the delight of Gilbert Powell's shareholders. One of the children, a boy, hung over his mother's shoulder, half asleep, half reading her messages.

I was thinking about that visit with my brother back in 2000. Haroun had been older and more worldly, having served in the army with C Company when Operation Uphold Democracy got rid of the military regime in Haiti, and after 9/11 he reenlisted for two tours in Afghanistan. But during those in-between years he'd fallen into a funk. He'd had trouble finding work and spent his free time reading political news and growing cynical. The idea of a trip to Western Sahara had been mine, casually tossed out over drinks, but it had given him something to work toward. He took it and ran. "Look, Abdul—before you disappear into some hole at Harvard, you need to see the world." I saw how energized the idea made him, and so I let him take control of the trip. He struck up conversations with strangers using our desert Arabic that, more often than not, earned us replies in English. To the cosmopolitan citizens of Rabat, I imagined, our slurred dialect made us sound like drug addicts. But that never slowed Haroun, and even after getting mugged and deciding to cut the trip short, not even having laid eyes on our ancestral homeland, he was already making plans for future trips.

My phone bleeped—Rashid was nexting me. Though I'd resisted, Laura had pushed for Rashid to have a phone. It was a way for her to always know where he was, which, in an age of school shootings, felt like a necessity. He wrote:

When are you getting home dad?

Soon, Monster. Late tomorrow or Friday. Everything ok?

Had a test. I was shook.

"Shook" was Rashid's word for describing any little trauma at school.

Did you do well on it?

Ok.

I suddenly realized what time it was in DC.

Wait. You're not allowed to use your phone in class!

Haha gotta go.

An hour before my connecting flight was scheduled to take off, over the speakers I heard the muezzin's call to prayer. Most travelers, including the grizzled patriarch, stayed where they were, but a few men got up and followed signs to the prayer rooms. After a moment's hesitation, I took my bag and joined them.

While that long-ago trip to Rabat had blunted my desire for adventure in the wider world, Haroun's was only enhanced. He became a student of Africa and after returning from Afghanistan went to work for Global Partners, advising Western corporations on the potential benefits and downsides of investing in the region. He traveled extensively, writing reports and sending me emails full of passion and excitement, littered with photos of camels and locals, tourist shots all. He got to know so much of West Africa that even after I started with CIA I sometimes quizzed him about on-the-ground knowledge our files sometimes got wrong. Guinea-Bissau, Sierra Leone, Liberia—he knew these hot spots like the back of his hand. And he was, in a way, the inverse of me. Where I needed silence and study to comprehend the world, he required noise and stink and human contact. Haroun was having the time of his life before it ended.

In August 2009, he was in Mauritania, working up an analysis of the feasibility of petroleum exploration in Taoudeni Basin, when he returned from the field to meet with his French clients. Nouakchott was one of his favorite capitals, an assessment I'd never understood. With Dakar to the south and Marrakesh to the north, why love a city so crushed by poverty that it couldn't even keep its harbor in working condition? But he found things to love, even choosing to rent rooms from locals rather than hide away in the air-conditioned modernity of the Semiramis or Le Diplomate. So on that day he took a taxi from run-down Sebkha to reach the French embassy.

August 8 was a hot day, though I suppose he was used to it. Outside the embassy, I understand, there was only a little foot traffic. A couple of gendarmes out jogging, a few passersby, and a young man, a jihadi, in a traditional boubou robe that hid his suicide belt.

The gendarmes and one passerby were injured. Only the terrorist and my brother were killed. That was ten years ago, and when I thought of West Africa I still pictured Haroun outside the French embassy, under the hot Mauritanian sun. I suppose I always will.

Beside strangers in the prayer room of Mohammed V International, I bowed and prostrated myself before God and, for the first time in many years, prayed.

4

Unlike Casablanca's international hub, Laayoune's tiny Hassan I, from above, looked ready to be swallowed by the Sahara. Despite the long-ago name change from Spanish to Western Sahara, the Arabic sign over the passenger terminal also read AEROPUERTO DE EL AAIÚN. Beyond, the flat, hard desert and dusty sky were ominous, and I wondered again why I had been picked for this particular mission.

The late-afternoon heat outside the airport was stifling, but I soon found a free driver smoking against a beaten-up Peugeot with functioning air-conditioning. He seemed surprised when I spoke the Hassānīya my parents had always insisted we use at home. He asked a lot of questions, wondering if I was part of the UN peacekeeping force, but I deflected with questions of my own, asking where the best meat pies could be had, the best markets, and the best cafés—subjects taxi drivers the world over can't help but elucidate on.

Outside the car, a desert wind was picking up, but the crowded salmon-pink buildings protected the streets from sand and sun. Locals filled the sidewalks, the colors of their robes touching something in my DNA. I felt a desire to call home and describe everything I saw to Rashid, to Laura. The feeling swelled so quickly that I even took out my phone before stopping myself. Paul had made clear that this wasn't allowed at the destination. And besides, I thought as I pocketed the phone again, the separation was probably good for us. Laura and I weren't trapped together in a small suburban house, walking on eggshells. We could breathe again, and perhaps with a couple of days' reprieve we would remember again why we'd chosen this life together.

That charmed feeling evaporated inside the sand-colored Hotel Parador, where the lobby was full of dozing foreigners who gave me weary looks. The MINURSO peacekeepers had brought with them the regular assortment of diplomats and carpetbaggers, and it looked like most of them had taken up residence in the Parador. Cynics and small-timers all—I'd spent a lot of my career reading reports from people like these, for whom the world was so much smaller than it really was, and I found their petty braggadocio tedious. Most analysts I knew felt this way, which was inevitable, I suppose, given our illusion of grander knowledge.

The hot water only lasted half my shower, and after washing I ate an energy bar while examining a map of the city, charting a route to the address Sally and Mel had given me before Paul sent me off to my cubicle to absorb whatever was still legible in that decimated file.

"A simple interview," they had told me. "Just the questions on the list."

"And if he doesn't want to talk?"

"Find out if it's just us he doesn't want to talk to, or if he's locking out the whole world."

So why not a phone call? Why not send these questions to someone already on location? Why send me, who had spent the last fourteen years behind a desk? Their answers had been equivocal, but the sad truth was the one I had suspected from the moment I first looked into their faces: They simply had no one else who could blend in as well as Abdul Ghali, their deskbound African.

I jumped at a knock at the door. *"Na-rħam?"* I called, folding the map.

"It's Collins," said an American voice.

Collins—yes, our local friend, very loosely attached to the UN mission. Paul had explained that Collins would set me up with anything I needed, which again raised the question: Why not just ask Collins to walk across town and do the interview? No one seemed to have a good answer for that.

I let in a balding man in knee-length shorts, tennis shoes, a Texas Tech baseball cap, and a dusty, sweat-stained jacket. We shook hands, and Collins looked around the room, sniffing. "Should've asked for a back-facing room. Gets noisy as hell here."

"I won't be here long enough for it to matter."

Collins grinned in a way I didn't like, then reached into the cargo pockets of his shorts. "We live in hope, man." He took out a flip phone and held it out to me. "My number's the only one in it." From his other pocket he took out a small semiautomatic pistol, checked the safety, and tossed it on the bed. "Colt 2000. Nine-millimeter, fifteen rounds. It'll get you where you're going."

I stared at it. "What's this for?"

"You're going into the slums, aren't you?"

"Yes, but I don't . . . I mean, I'm not—"

"Look, kid. It's there to make you feel better. You take that out, and whoever's giving you trouble is going to think twice. I hope to hell you don't pull the trigger—I don't need that kind of paperwork. But take it. Okay?"

I nodded even though my brain was saying no. After a day of traveling in solitude, this sudden bluster was disconcerting, and the addition of a pistol made me think again of 2009, and my brother. It shouldn't have—he'd died in another country and had only sung the praises of Laayoune—but it did. Maybe because we'd never been able to bury him ourselves. His body, we were told, lay on the outskirts of Bissau, in a cemetery only our father had had the heart to visit.

Still not touching the gun, I said, "You're the one who found him?"

"No. And it doesn't exactly reflect well on me that after two years in this dump I didn't notice our little newcomer. I mean, *him* of all people. He apparently made a *phone call* to the States. Stupid slip."

I wondered about that.

Collins furrowed his brow, eyeballing me. "Look, all you have to worry about is your twenty questions. Okay?"

"And you?"

"Me? Don't worry about me."

It wasn't him I was worried about. "You're not coming?"

"Sure," he said. "I'm coming. But you're not going to see me. You see me, *they* see me. And we don't want to scare anyone off. HQ's been looking months for this bastard. Let's not lose him."

"But if I need—"

"That," he said, pointing to the flip phone still in my hand. "You call, I come. No more than a minute or two. And unlike you, I don't have a problem carrying." To prove his point, he opened his sweat-stained jacket to reveal a shoulder holster and a worn pistol grip. Then he considered me a moment, judgment all over him, and said, "You don't need to be scared, okay? Things they say about this guy? He probably made them up himself. His dad was KGB; making up shit is in his blood."

"What do they say about him?"

Collins opened his mouth, then shut it. "How much are you read in on?"

"Not a lot. Ties to the Massive Brigade."

"That's it?"

I shrugged.

He cursed under his breath and stepped away, toward the windows, flexing his fists. "They send you here without . . ." He shook his head, unwilling to finish the sentence, then turned back to me. Made a smile that filled me with unease. "Maybe it's better you don't know. Why fuck with your nerves, right? Keep your calm."

At no point during this conversation had I felt calm about anything, but now Collins had pushed it to the emotional equivalent of nails scratching a chalkboard. So I took a baby step closer, looked him square in the eyes, and said, "Collins, I need you to tell me exactly what the hell I'm walking into here."

5

The sun was almost gone when I finally faced the busy evening streets. A few vendors approached, and in hard-edged Arabic I sent them away. My face and speech might have helped me blend in, but no one had given me a new set of clothes, so the best impression I gave was of a local boy who had grown rich in the West. And why else would I have returned but to spread the wealth? I was a magnet.

The western wind, coming off the Atlantic and pushing inland from Foum el-Oued across twenty-five miles of desert, had cleaned some of the dust from the air, and as I passed teahouses and fruit vendors I felt another urge to call home. At the very least, I could take the same kinds of tourist shots my brother had once taken, so that I could show them off to my family later. But no—if Collins, who I assumed was tailing me at a distance, saw me pulling out my phone, there was no telling what would happen.

I chose to walk the entire distance, about an hour's stroll. I wasn't worried about taxi drivers asking questions or collecting records of my time here; I simply wanted to breathe in the culture that I'd always held at arm's length. I might have spoken my parents' language at home, but as soon as I was out the front door I'd tried to become like my friends, a child of McDonald's and MTV, of fads and convenience. To my younger self, American culture was superior simply because my friends knew of no other, and there was no way I was going to draw them into mine by dragging them home to our bi-level shrine to West Africa. My mother's Daraa robes and dishes of goat meifrisa would only scare them.

Even as a child I was painfully aware of my limits.

Now I was in a land that I knew but did not know, and I pressed on, thinking of my destination.

"So you know about the Library," Collins said, and when I shook my head I thought he was going to punch a hole in the hotel's stucco wall. "Okay," he said, calming himself. "Tell me they at least told you he works for the UN."

My nod provoked a happy sigh.

"Small favors, right? Well, remember what I said—Weaver's dad used to work for the Russians. But then the old man moved to the UN, where he created this thing called the Library. His thinking, we gather, was that the intelligence agencies of the first world countries have a monopoly on what is known and not known in the world. And we work together—us and Israel and the UK, Russia and China, all of us together—to filter and alter intelligence to suit our own ends. So he put together his own outfit, the Library, and hid it deep inside the United Nations. Inside UNESCO."

I tried to picture it but couldn't. "The UN can barely fund its central air-conditioning, much less an intelligence agency."

Collins shrugged. "That part's a mystery. But however they did it, it functioned. And when the old man died back in oh-eight, his boy took it over. Been running it ever since. And from all accounts it worked well, completely under the radar, until it was blown back in October. Same time he disappeared."

"Blown?"

"Wide open," Collins said.

"Then why haven't I heard about it?"

Collins wagged a dirty fingernail at me. "Not to the plebes, man. That's seventh-floor knowledge. Don't know who uncovered it first, but soon everyone knew—us, the Europeans, the Chinese . . . hell, even the Iranians got word of it. And do you know why it was blown?"

I didn't.

"The Library stopped collecting intelligence; it started *creating* intelligence. It became an agency of active measures. Liquidating people. Remember Lou Braxton?"

I did. Braxton had been a Silicon Valley darling, founder of Where4, Nexus's only serious competitor in the encrypted communications sector, until a couple of years ago when he died on a Beijing–San Francisco flight. "He died of cardiac arrest," I said.

"With a full gram of sodium fluoroacetate in his system." Off my ignorant look, he said, "Compound 1080—it's used to kill pests. The company kept that quiet, but it didn't help. A year later Where4 was bankrupt."

"The Library murdered him? Why?"

Collins asked. "Who's to say? They're *global*. You hear of Joseph Keller?"

"He's in the questions. Number eight—explain the circumstances of his death."

Collins looked disappointed. "That's all? Well, he was a British accountant. Worked for the Russians—MirGaz. We heard he had a side-gig laundering money for the Massive Brigade, so we put out a Red Notice on him. Then in October, when everything was blowing up, Paris cops found him buried in a park out in the burbs. The Library killing off its weak link. That's the theory."

"Jesus."

"They're even connected to piracy."

Though I felt stupid saying it, I couldn't help but blurt, "*Piracy?* That makes no sense."

"Not to me either," Collins said. "But all that? Someone was bound to notice. Us, the Europeans, the Russians, the Chinese. *Everyone* noticed. And everyone tried to take it *down*."

"Did they succeed?"

"I suppose so—why else would the Library's director be hiding out in this hellhole?"

"And the Massive Brigade?" I asked.

Collins opened his hands. "Weaver protected them in the past—that's documented. Whatever you do, don't underestimate him, okay? He's hard as shit."

There was no discernible change when I entered the slums of what Collins called a hellhole. The old Spanish architecture remained, and the dilapidated windows and shallow terraces and crumbling façades lining the narrow streets were just as they had been a few blocks back. But now there were more children running around columns and through alleys, slipping in and out of shadows, while others sat on steps and stared at me as I passed. It was unnerving, but when the fear crept up I thought of Haroun, who had for years traversed places far more ominous than this without anything more than a scratch. He hadn't been killed by the greed of the world's poor but by a blind religious fury that could have found him in Paris or London or New York.

I've always had a head for geography, and I reached the three-story walkup on Boulevard Al Hizam Al Kabir without a misstep. Like many other buildings I'd passed, it was dead looking, and I gazed up at the shuttered windows, thinking about the children around me, watching from a safe distance. I thought of Collins, watching from among them, and I thought of the uncomfortable gun in my waistband at the base of my back. And I thought that this truly was not part of my job description. I looked at data, and I interpreted it. I did not go searching for the data; that was what people like Collins were paid to do.

In the darkness I found a light switch on a timer, and in its bright glare the stairwell was surprisingly cool, dark, and clean. The banister shook when I touched it, so I left it alone as I ascended to the second floor. Off to the left a family was making noise, and a radio played a Haifa Wehbe hit. Weaver's apartment—identified by a handwritten *4* on the door—was to my right, and when the timer ended darkness fell. I stood blind, listening to the high melody of Arabic pop but hearing nothing from behind number 4. Then I stepped forward and knocked three times.

Silence. I considered walking away. A man exiles himself in Western Sahara—that means he's not interested in talking. And from what little I knew from the file, and from the mysterious nuggets Collins had given me, Milo Weaver wasn't the kind of man who would talk if he wasn't interested in talking.

But I stayed, if only because I didn't want to return to those warm, dusty streets so quickly. I knocked again and said, "Hello?"

To my left, a door opened, spilling light into the stairwell, and a small girl peered out at me. The noise and aroma of a family meal wafted out with the Arabic dance music, then an indecipherable father's shout; the child shut the door. Then number 4 opened quickly, accompanied by dim light, and a sunburned face peered out at me. A scatter of bristle, some of it gray, reached to his cheekbones, and there was gray around his ears. Big, bruised eyes.

Looking nothing like his photos, yet exactly like his photos. Sandals, linen pants, a light-colored shirt he was still buttoning.

"Milo Weaver?" I said.

A pleasant enough smile crossed his face, and with a voice rough from disuse, he said, "Well, you certainly took your time."

Rana Faure

OLEN STEINHAUER, the *New York Times* bestselling author of twelve novels, is a Dashiell Hammett Prize winner and a two-time Edgar Award finalist, and has been nominated for the Anthony, Ian Fleming Steel Dagger, Ellis Peters Historical Dagger, Macavity, and Barry awards. He is also the creator of the Epix TV series *Berlin Station*. He was raised in Virginia and now divides his time between New York and Budapest.

READ THE ENTIRE MILO WEAVER SERIES BY BESTSELLING AUTHOR

OLEN STEINHAUER

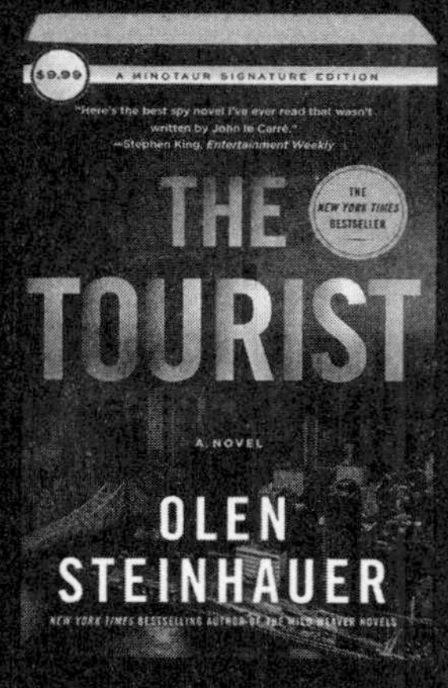

ISBN: 978-1-250-62209-9
E-ISBN: 978-1-4299-7718-0

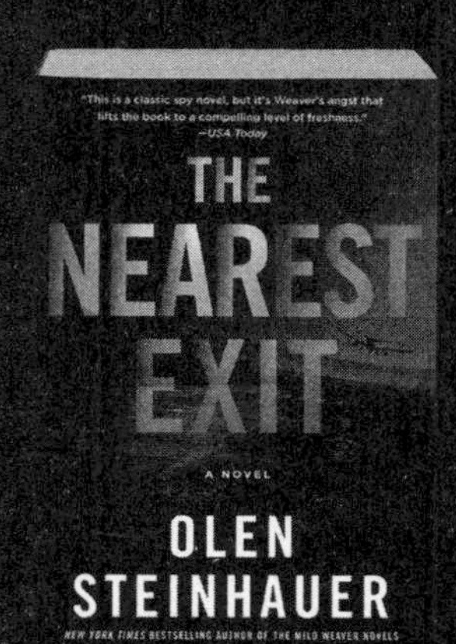

ISBN: 978-1-250-62210-5
E-ISBN: 978-1-4299-2723-9

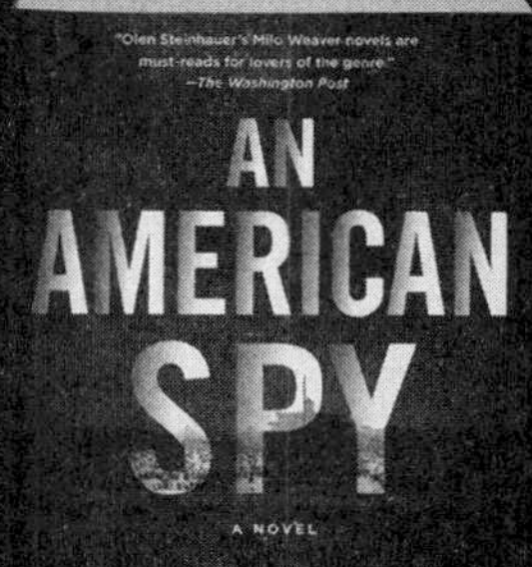

ISBN: 978-1-250-62211-2
E-ISBN: 978-1-4299-5044-2

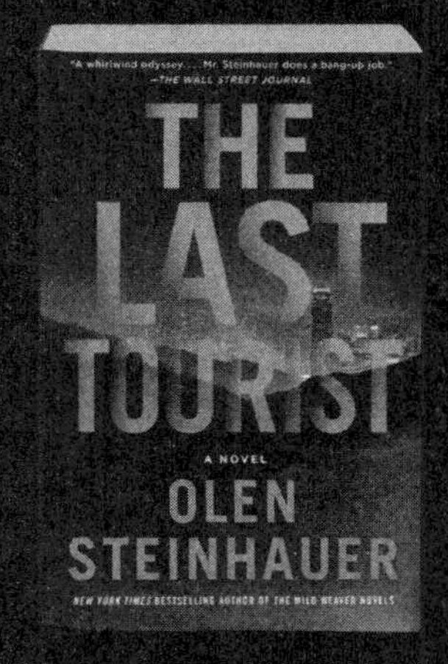

ISBN: 978-1-250-03619-3
E-ISBN: 978-1-250-03620-9

READ THE ENTIRE YALTA BOULEVARD SEQUENCE

"[Steinhauer's] people are real, the crimes genuine, and he is telling larger truths about that era, making it unusually accessible."

—David Halberstam, *Los Angeles Times*

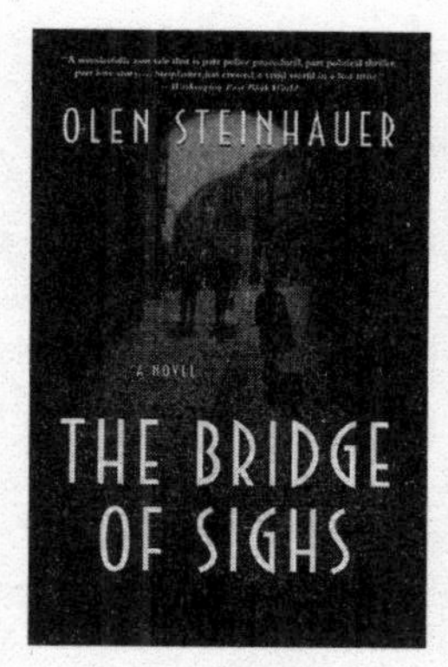

ISBN: 978-0-312-32601-2
E-ISBN: 978-1-4299-8116-3

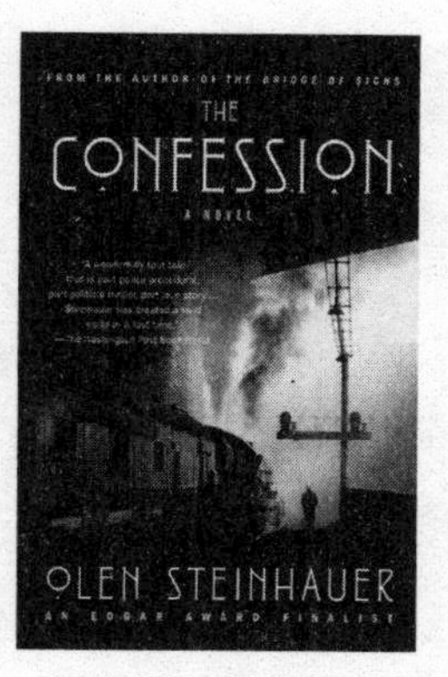

ISBN: 978-0-312-33815-2
E-ISBN: 978-1-4299-8118-7

ISBN: 978-0-312-33203-7
E-ISBN: 978-1-4299-4013-9

ISBN: 978-0-312-33205-1
E-ISBN: 978-1-4299-0922-8

ISBN: 978-0-312-37486-0
E-ISBN: 978-1-4299-7474-5

Available wherever books are sold.

 MINOTAUR BOOKS www.MinotaurBooks.com

LISTEN TO

THE LAST TOURIST

AN *AUDIOFILE* BEST AUDIOBOOK OF 2020

READ BY AUDIE AWARD-WINNING ACTOR DAVID PITTU

"[David] Pittu juggles an impressive range of characters and accents. Listeners will admire his skill as he creates an unsettling, immersive experience."

—*AUDIOFILE*

AVAILABLE ON CD AND AS A DIGITAL DOWNLOAD

AND DON'T MISS OLEN STEINHAUER'S OTHER AUDIOBOOKS

The Middleman

All the Old Knives

The Cairo Affair

An American Spy

The Nearest Exit

Visit MacmillanAudio.com for audio samples and more!
Follow us on Facebook, Instagram, and Twitter.